These twin sisters have shared everything
in their lives—but they didn't plan on
becoming pregnant at the same time,
until they find themselves…

Unexpectedly Expecting

Last month we met Lianne.
She hasn't found Mr. Right, but she's
longing to have a baby before it's too late!

**Her sister, Annalise, has the perfect life—
a sexy husband, a fabulous home and
a great career. But when she made her
wedding vows, she also made a pact
with her husband: theirs would
always be a family of two!**

Dear Reader,

I've always been fascinated by twins, wondering how it would feel to have someone in my life who looked exactly like I do. I have heard of a special bond between twins, and so began to explore the idea of twin sisters who want different things out of life and yet end up in similar situations.

Lianne O'Mallory is the single twin who longs for a baby. She has a medical problem that's getting worse. A ticking clock, much earlier than most women face it, adds to the urgency of becoming pregnant. But she's particular. She doesn't want just anyone to father her baby. She makes a list of the appealing attributes she'd like for the father of her child, and is shocked when her boss reads it and volunteers.

Lianne's twin, Annalise, has been married for five years. Early in her relationship with her husband, they decided not to have children. Unexpectedly, Annalise becomes pregnant, and suddenly her plans for the future change drastically. The only problem is her husband's views have not changed.

United, the sisters work out the solutions to their situations, which promise a happy future for all.

Though each twin has her own story, they are closely intertwined, just as twins are.

If you are a twin, I hope I captured the special bond you have with your double. If you're not a twin, come explore that special tie in these stories.

All the best,

Barbara

BARBARA McMAHON

Parents in Training

Unexpectedly Expecting

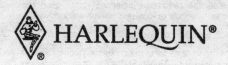

HARLEQUIN®

TORONTO • NEW YORK • LONDON
AMSTERDAM • PARIS • SYDNEY • HAMBURG
STOCKHOLM • ATHENS • TOKYO • MILAN • MADRID
PRAGUE • WARSAW • BUDAPEST • AUCKLAND

ISBN-13: 978-0-373-17523-9
ISBN-10:   0-373-17523-X

PARENTS IN TRAINING

First North American Publication 2008.

Copyright © 2008 by Barbara McMahon.

www.eHarlequin.com

Printed in U.S.A.

Barbara McMahon was born and raised in the South, but settled in California after spending a year flying around the world for an international airline. After settling down to raise a family and work for a computer firm, she began writing when her children started school. Now, feeling fortunate in being able to realize a long-held dream of quitting her day job and writing full-time, Barbara has moved with her husband to the Sierra Nevada mountains of California, where she finds her desire to write is stronger than ever. With the beauty of the mountains visible from her windows and the pace of life slower than that of the hectic San Francisco Bay Area, where they previously resided, she finds more time than ever to think up stories and characters and share them with others through writing. Barbara loves to hear from readers. You can reach her at P.O. Box 977, Pioneer, CA 95666-0977, U.S.A.

Readers can also contact Barbara at her Web site, www.barbaramcmahon.com.

Jessie McMahon, spread your wings and fly!
Love from Mom-Mom

CHAPTER ONE

ANNALISE stared at the plastic stick, stunned to see the positive indicator. It took a moment or two to register. The plus meant she was pregnant. Impossible.

She carefully wrapped the kit in the brown paper bag she'd brought it home in and stuffed into the small bathroom trash container. Then she pulled it out. Too obvious. She carried it to the kitchen and stuffed it into that trash. Picking up the container, she went to the hallway incinerator chute and emptied the telltale evidence.

Fifteen minutes later, she stood in McClellan's Drugstore buying another brand of pregnancy-test kit. Without a second thought she bought two. No sense taking chances on a faulty reading.

When both of those kits confirmed what she secretly wouldn't admit she'd known, she went to flop down on the edge of the bed. This couldn't be the worst thing that had happened to her since marrying Dominic, but it seemed like it. His sentiments played in her mind. They'd had a discussion about having children just recently, when her twin sister announced she was pregnant.

Lianne had been trying. Annalise had not.

She *so* did not need this.

Dominic was going to hit the roof. Things had been a bit testy between them for the last few weeks. Thinking back, she wondered if it coincided with her confiding in him Lianne's quest to have a baby before it was too late. He had said unequivocally that he was satisfied with their marriage. They'd discussed having children years ago and decided not to. He had not changed his view.

Annalise wasn't sure how she felt, but she knew when he learned she was pregnant he was going to explode.

Annalise felt a bit overwhelmed herself. She'd never pictured herself a mother. She had better readjust her thinking. How far along was she? There was no way she could pinpoint the date of conception, but she tried to remember her last period. Maybe two months ago? Could she expect the baby to arrive in seven months? Ohmygod—how was she going to tell Dominic?

She had to tell him soon. Try to minimize the fall-out. Convince him this would be a good thing. Only how she would accomplish that was a mystery right now— she herself wasn't so sure she wanted a child.

So when to tell Dominic? Tonight they were hosting a cocktail party for twenty-four. Should she get hold of him before? Or wait? Should she lead up to it or just blurt it out? She hoped the right words came. Rising, she went to the phone in the living room and called his cell number. It rolled to the message center. *Damn.* He must be in a high-level meeting to have turned his phone off. The seconds ticked by. She replaced the receiver without leaving him a message. Maybe he'd get home early and she'd tell him then.

Or maybe wait until everyone had left, so there'd be no tension at the party. That was what she'd do. Taking a deep breath, Annalise tried to quell the flutters in her stomach. He had to be reasonable about this. After all, it took two to make a baby. It wasn't as if she'd deliberately tried to become pregnant. She was not following in Lianne's footsteps. But something told her Dominic was not going to be reasonable.

They'd had several heated discussions about having a family in the last few weeks. Every time, Dominic had been stubbornly adamant—against the idea. She hadn't pushed. She knew what living in a large family was like. And she'd agreed years ago when he'd brought up marriage, that a childless one suited her just fine. Fresh from the chaos of a large family, the idea of only the two of them doing what they wanted had sounded to her like perfection.

Still, a small smiled played around her mouth. *They were going to have a baby.*

How amazing—she and her twin were pregnant at the same time.

Now she just had to make her husband see what a wonderful thing this would be.

The one time Annalise really wanted to speak to her husband, he was late. The party had already begun when he dashed in, making excuses, greeting their guests with the confidence of a well-respected man. She knew the instant he entered. Whenever he was near it was as if she had a special sixth sense that instantly recognized his presence.

She went to greet him, happy to see he wasn't going to be so late as to be awkward. Greeting their first guests without him had been bad enough.

"Hello, darling," she said, with a wide smile.

"Sweetheart," he said, giving her a quick kiss and turning almost simultaneously to greet Ben Waters.

Once Dominic had put down his briefcase, he began to walk through the large living room, greeting guests, apologizing for being late, stopping with one group or another to chat for a while.

Annalise knew she couldn't tell him her important news until the last guest had left, so she resigned herself to a long evening of anticipation and dread. Normally she loved to entertain. They had a wide, eclectic group of friends. She watched Dominic as he shook hands with Congressman Peters. The congressman's wife was very shy. Annalise had invited her sister Bridget to the party to meet Judy Peters. They both were avid gardeners, and Annalise knew they'd hit it off.

"Lovely to see you again, my dear," Sheila Simpson said, coming up to Annalise. "So nice to have an event to attend where I know everyone and like them. Honestly, some of the receptions and parties we have to attend are too dull and boring for words." She laughed and chatted. Her husband was with the world bank, and Annalise knew Sheila loved parties of all types. She couldn't imagine her friend finding anything boring.

"Here's Karen. I was just saying how lovely this party is," Sheila said, when the wife of one of the British attachés joined them. "You look radiant."

Annalise smiled at Karen, who was very obviously pregnant. Annalise relished her secret—soon she'd be showing the world *she* carried a baby. She hugged her friend. "How are you feeling?"

"Fabulous, now that the morning sickness has passed. I thought I'd have to move into the bath for a few months. Yuck. But now everything is terrific."

Sheila laughed and complimented her on her dress.

"I feel huge, and I'm still three months away. Imagine how large I'll be by the end. Oh, the baby just kicked," Karen said, with a startled smile.

"Really?" Annalise stared at her friend's protruding stomach. "Can I feel?"

"Of course—that's one of the best parts. Here." Karen took her hand and placed it to the side of her stomach. A moment later, Annalise felt a definite kick.

"Ah! Amazing." Involuntarily, she looked for Dominic. Would he soon be placing his hands on her stomach to feel their baby move?

Dominic glanced across the room and met Annalise's eyes. She smiled at him, then turned back to Karen Reynolds. A pregnant Karen. Annalise had her palm against the pregnant woman's belly. There was a soft smile on her face. For a moment, the world seemed to stand still. The topic of a baby had risen more in the last two months than in the previous five years of their marriage. His mouth went dry. He did not wish to discuss having a family again. He'd made his view known over and over. When they had first discussed marriage, as seniors at university, both had agreed—no children.

The topic had not risen again until Annalise's twin became pregnant. Now it seemed every time he turned around he was seeing pregnant women, hearing about someone else having another child. He couldn't do that. Not again.

Deliberately turning, so he didn't have to see Annalise, he caught the thread of a conversation between two guests and tried to concentrate.

Annalise worked in real estate, specializing in homes in the northwest section of Washington, catering to embassy personnel and members of Congress. It was a rewarding job that enabled her to take a week off here and there whenever Dominic got a choice overseas assignment. It also enabled her to meet a wide variety of people. Many of whom became friends.

Dominic worked for a computer firm which specialized in troubleshooting high-end computer mainframes. His most recent trip, to England, had been to work on one with the Bank of England. The challenges were dramatic, but he thrived on solving complex problems. He was often given the most difficult ones, and usually turned things around within a few days of arriving on site. Which then gave he and Annalise time to sightsee and shop.

With his contacts through the "computer-repair business," as he called it, and her contacts from houses sold or listed, they had a wide variety of friends and acquaintances. Annalise loved giving parties with an assortment of guests. It made the evenings so interesting and fun. She could move from an argument between opposites about the world bank situation, to discussions about tourism in Florida, to hearing how an artist had fared at the latest showing of her work, all while circling her own living room. Tonight was no exception.

Some time later, Dominic poured himself another glass of wine. Glancing up, he heard Annalise's laugh. For a moment, he just gazed at her. She was lovely. He'd been attracted to her from the first moment they met. It wasn't only her looks that had appealed, but her manner, as well. She was confident and assured in any situation he'd seen her in. Friendly and genuinely interested in people, she loved to entertain and kept up with a wide circle of friends. She was so unlike his mother had been. Involuntarily a memory rose. His mother had looked far older than her years, and had worked nonstop as a clerk in a convenience store to keep their home, constantly arguing with his father about new furniture. He couldn't remember his parents ever entertaining friends. Annalise made it look so easy. His mother would have been horrified, and probably terrified at the assortment of people present. He frowned at the thought. He didn't need the past intruding.

Maybe he should have expected it to with all the talk about pregnancy. He was not cut out to be a father. He knew it, and if the subject arose again, Annalise would have to accept the fact. Even Phyllis—

He turned away from the thought. He was married to a lovely, successful woman. Their future together was bright. He'd fought his way out of the life he'd once lived and was never going back.

The evening was winding down when Dominic finally got time to catch up with Annalise. She seemed quieter than usual. When she thought no one was watching, her smile faded. They'd returned from London four days ago—maybe she was still suffering jet lag.

The trip had been a success, both from a business point of view and as a few days' down time. He shared Annalise's love for London. Though he was partial to Rome, as well. Part of the excitement of his job was never knowing where the next assignment would be. He relished the travel, and the opportunity to pit his wits and brain against the problems that arose with various software and computer usage. Most of the time it was silly mistakes. Occasionally industrial espionage or sabotage lay behind the difficulties.

The best part, however, was seeing the world and getting paid for it. Quite a change from his rather bleak childhood in a small Pennsylvania mill town.

He moved toward his wife and smiled. She was beautiful. Her glossy brown hair was pulled back from her face. Her complexion was like peaches and cream. No wonder writers waxed poetic about such skin. It made him yearn to reach out across the room and rub his fingertip across it, feeling its silky softness.

Suddenly he was glad the first of the guests were leaving. He moved to Annalise's side to bid them good-night.

"Enjoyed seeing you again," he said as he shook Ted's hand, kissed Karen on the cheek. It figured the pregnant couple would be the first to leave. He remembered how tired Phyllis had been for months. He could feel himself tense at the memory.

"Come see us before the baby is born. It'll be hectic after that," Ted said.

"We'd love to," Annalise said. She gave Karen a hug, and then Ted. "Keep safe."

Soon the exodus began. Within a half-hour, the last guest had left.

"Wonderful party," he said casually, throwing his arm around her shoulder as they turned to survey the catering staff beginning the clean-up.

"I like this caterer. I think I'll try them again when we give a dinner party. They have an interesting menu selection. Maybe next time I'll mix European with Asian." She looked at him. "Are you listening to me?"

"Of course."

Her voice was soft and feminine. He liked listening to her—especially late at night, when they were in bed with the lights out. He could close his eyes and listen to her for hours. Not that they talked all that much in bed after dark. He smiled. They'd be in bed soon.

"Bridget made an instant rapport with the new congressman's wife."

Dominic nodded. He remembered her telling him she'd invited them after she'd sold them a home. And the Campbells had brought a house guest—a sheikh—who had graced them with his presence and had turned out to be wildly funny. Who would have thought? Everyone had stayed far longer than predicted—a sure sign all had enjoyed the evening as much as he and Annalise had.

She relaxed against him. "I'm so tired. It was fun, though, wasn't it? Did you get to hear Sheikh Ramaise's commentary on American cowboys?"

"I did. He's an excellent storyteller."

"I stand in amazement at his command of English. I could never learn Arabic."

"You don't need to. But he needs English to represent his country to ours."

"Umm." She walked to the sofa and sank down.

"Tired?"

"A bit."

But she looked keyed up, on edge.

Members of the catering staff moved efficiently through the apartment, clearing away the debris from the event. Soon the living room was back to its normal state. Dominic heard them working in the kitchen. As soon as they left, he was going to take his wife to bed.

Dominic shed his jacket and tie, then loosened his shirt collar. "Did you hear Jack Simpson talking about the problems with that country in South America?"

She shook her head, waiting.

Dominic poured them each a brandy, handed her a glass and sat beside her on the sofa while he gave a brief recap. He noticed she put her glass on the coffee table and didn't pick it up.

"We're leaving now," the representative from the catering firm said, coming to the kitchen doorway. "All cleaned up."

With a quick glance at Annalise, Dominic rose. "I'll check them out and pay them," he said.

She nodded, closing her eyes.

"Good group tonight. Everyone seemed to mesh," Dominic said when he returned.

She opened her eyes and smiled. "We'll have to do it again soon."

"Next weekend, if we're home, do you want to catch the National Symphony Orchestra at the Kennedy Center?" he asked, taking his tie and jacket from the chair.

Annalise nodded. Stifling a yawn, she said, "That sounds good. I have to call Lianne tomorrow," she said.

Dominic didn't reply. He crossed the room to switch off one lamp. The one thing he'd never completely understood about Annalise was her close tie with her sister Lianne. It was a twin thing, he was sure. They communicated almost daily, had done all their lives—even when they'd lived in different cities and gone to different universities.

He liked Lianne, but he wondered what the two of them had to talk about all the time.

"How's she doing?" he asked. He didn't want to know, but his wife would expect him to ask.

"Still thrilled to be pregnant."

He hoped that was one twin trait they didn't share. When he and Annalise had first met, at Georgetown

University, they'd hit it off immediately. He'd loved being with her, enjoyed her enthusiasm about everything. She'd been so different from his high-school girlfriend, who had been needy and demanding. Annalise had been a breath of fresh air, and he'd moved in on her like a hunter on prey.

Before long, they'd become a couple, then engaged, and had married right after graduation. Having children did not play in his plans. His own father was a shining example of the opposite of Father-of-the-Year. The apple didn't fall far from the tree. He knew from the past he was not cut out to be a father.

He didn't voice his concern that Annalise was only toying with the idea of a child because her sister was pregnant. They lived separate lives, for all they were close. Lianne had recently married, for one thing; he and Annalise had been married for five years. Lianne worked as an analyst in a security firm; Annalise was more independent as a real-estate agent.

The twins were from a family of eleven children. They were next to oldest, with two older boys also twins. Even after knowing the members of her family for half a dozen years, he was amazed at the sheer chaotic nature of holiday gatherings, and the amazing patience of their father, Patrick O'Mallory. Dominic had been an only child, and happy to leave home when he'd had the chance. He was used to the O'Mallory celebrations now, but was always glad to leave for the quieter, more tranquil apartment they owned.

He couldn't understand Lianne's burning desire for a child. It was totally foreign to him.

He reached out and caught Annalise's hand, bringing it to his mouth for a quick kiss. "I'm telling the schedulers to try for a New York assignment next time. There are some new plays we haven't seen. Might as well have the company pick up some of the tab."

"You do that. And I'll see if I can sell a home or two so we can afford the best seats."

He wasn't worried about Annalise selling property. She was a natural at it. Her sunny disposition and genuine liking for people shone through when she acquired clients. They knew instinctively that she would find the best property available for them.

And they could afford the best seats in any theater without another sale. After a childhood of deprivation, the one thing Dominic made sure of was that there was plenty of money for unexpected expenditure. They had a very healthy savings and investment plan. Never again would he experience the hardship of his early years.

"Ready for bed?"

"Not yet. Sit down. I have something to tell with you," she said.

He sat on the sofa beside her.

Annalise took a deep breath.

"What's up?" he asked.

"I'm pregnant." She looked at him, as if gauging his reaction.

Dominic didn't believe he'd heard the words at first.

His worst nightmare.

For a moment, he was eighteen again, and hearing the dreaded words from Phyllis Evans. Life as he had planned it had changed with those two words. He had never wanted to hear them again. And now Annalise was staring at him, having uttered the words that struck dread into his heart.

"How did that happen?" he asked evenly, holding on to control by a thread. Anger began to build. They were always very careful, so had Annalise had a change of heart about having a child?

It was Lianne's influence. He knew it. He had always been distrustful of the tie between the twins. He had felt excluded on more than one occasion when the two of them had been together. Twins shared a special bond, one a husband couldn't ever penetrate. But for Annalise to change their lives so completely without even talking about it with him was beyond anything.

"The usual way," she said, trying for flippancy but sounding tentative.

He gazed at her in disbelief. He took a breath, trying to get the anger under control. She looked wary, watching him carefully. Well, she should. He wanted to smash something. To tip the table over and storm out of the room. He had been through this once before—with disastrous results. He could not go through it again.

Clamping down on his emotions, he tried to think. But the only thought that ricocheted around his mind was the fact they were bringing a child into the world and life as he knew it—as he liked it—would end forever.

He stood, paced to the window, clenching his hands into fists. He felt the room close in on him. "Dammit, Annalise, we talked about this. More than once. I. Do. Not. Want. Children. What part of that do you not understand?"

"I understand it all. But I didn't do anything to become pregnant. If you'll remember, we agreed before we were married that a childless marriage would be a wonderful thing. But you and I both know the only perfect birth control is abstinence, and that's not something we practice. You and me together made a baby. It'll take some adjusting, but I'm sure we'll be happy when the baby's born. We can make it work. I know we can."

He turned and faced her. It was like looking at a total stranger. "Is this a twin thing? Lianne is pregnant, so you had to be, too?"

"No." She was quiet for a moment. "I'm as stunned as you. I didn't plan on this. You can't think that. It'll change everything."

"You've got that right. We like to travel. A kid will mean no more jumping up at the last moment and taking off somewhere. There would be so much to tie us down. What kind of life do you envision for us with a baby in the mix? Or when he's six, and in school for most of the year? Or as a teenager, giving untold grief? This is the last thing we need!"

"We'll adapt. I only found out this afternoon. I haven't had a chance to do anything but try to get used to the idea myself," she said. "And if my folks can get through eleven kids, I'm sure we can manage one."

"How did you find out? Did you see a doctor?"

"No, I took a home pregnancy test."

For a moment, a glimmer of hope rose. "Take another one. They aren't one hundred percent."

"I tried three. Every one showed positive."

He hit the wall with his fist. "Dammit, Annalise, we weren't going to have children. We agreed to that." He glared at her. "I like the life we have. If I had wanted it changed, I would have said something."

She stood and put her hands on her hips, glaring at him. "I wasn't planning anything except to go on as we've been. Do you think I want to be tied down, unable to go off on a moment's notice? I love traveling. I never was able to go anywhere but the shore when we were children. Don't blame me for this. It takes two."

"So how did it happen?"

"How should I know? Something didn't work, obviously. Now we have a situation we have to deal with. We'll have to adjust our thinking."

"I don't want to adjust." God, he knew he sounded petulant and stubborn. But if she knew the full story— He blanked the thought. The last thing he wanted was for anyone to know the full story.

"Well, tough. There it is. What else do you suggest?" Her wariness had faded. She glared at him.

He couldn't think. He was furious with the news. And afraid of the past repeating itself.

"Hell, I don't know. Why not consult your precious sister?" he said, and strode from the room. Snatching a jacket, he headed for the door. "I don't want the baby."

The moment he said the words, he cringed. How cold it sounded—especially when it echoed what he'd said years ago. And look at that result. Guilt and grief played out. He knew intellectually he had not caused the outcome, but secretly he'd always believed he had. He'd never planned to bring a child into the world, disrupting the life he'd carefully built. He still had challenges he wanted to meet, places to visit. This would change everything—if he let it.

Annalise stared at him for a long moment. "How could anyone not want a baby?" she asked. "Granted, we didn't plan on one. But now that it's on the way, we will love this child."

"There are millions of people on the planet who do not want children," he said. It wasn't only the thought of a baby but the betrayal he felt at his wife's becoming pregnant. That was exactly what he felt—betrayed.

"Well, there's not much to be done about it now," she said, turning and heading down the hall.

A moment later, Dominic heard the slam of the bedroom door.

What a mess. He let himself out of the apartment. He reached the sidewalk and turned south. Blocks away lay the Mall, with the Lincoln Monument at one end and the Capitol at the other. On the other side of the Mall was the Tidal Basin. The open space would allow him some breathing room. He felt claustrophobic in the apartment. Like the walls were closing in on him. Like the past was returning. He needed freedom.

He could hear his father's voice echoing—how having a kid had kept him from doing all he wanted. He'd blamed Dominic's mother for getting pregnant and forcing him to marry her. For having a child that needed care, which had kept his father from traveling the world and living life to the fullest. The arguments had been endless, and Dominic remembered every one.

He'd felt the same way when Phyllis had told him she was pregnant. Eighteen, just graduated from high school, and all his plans for the future down the drain. They'd been sweethearts in high school, but once graduation had come, he'd had his ticket to freedom. Only, Phyllis's news had changed that. He'd done the right thing by marrying her. Then he'd gone to work at the mill. Same as his father. History repeating itself.

Only, when there'd been a reprieve, he'd grabbed it.

He'd sworn he would never get in that position again. He liked his job, combining computer work with travel. He liked Annalise, beautiful, sophisticated. Not tired all the time and scared like Phyllis had been. This pregnancy had the power to change everything—just like before.

* * *

Annalise sat on the edge of the bed, frustrated and angry. She had *not* made a decision for them. She'd never had daydreams about having babies. How could he think that? Okay, maybe she had brought up the subject when Lianne began talking about having a baby. But when Dominic had said unequivocally no, she'd accepted they'd stay childless.

Granted, she'd enjoyed holding her sister Mary Margaret's babies when they'd been small, but she'd always been relieved to give them back to Mama when they cried.

Now she was going to have a baby of her own. One she couldn't hand back when it cried. She hoped Dominic got used to the idea fast. Sure, there'd be some adjustments. She rubbed her tummy, hoping the baby didn't feel the turmoil. Why couldn't Dominic be like Tray, her sister's husband, and overjoyed at the thought of a child?

Why should he? She wasn't as ecstatic as Lianne. This would mean major compromises when before they'd lived life on their own terms. She had to get used to the idea herself.

Still, having a baby was a good thing. She'd better hold on to that thought. There was no going back now. They both had solid careers, made enough money to live comfortably and provide for a child. It wasn't what they'd planned, but it wasn't the end of the world like Dominic made it seem. He had to come around. He *had* to.

The next morning when Annalise awoke, she realized Dominic had never come to bed. Had he even returned home? She put on her robe and went down the hall. The apartment was quiet. He was not in the living room, nor the kitchen. She went to the den and peered in. He was stretched out on the recliner, asleep, still wearing the clothes he'd had on last night. The computer screen scrolled its screensaver. Had he been working and fallen asleep? Or had he deliberately stayed away?

"Dominic?" she called softly.

He didn't move.

Annalise went to shower and dress. Then she went to the kitchen to prepare breakfast. She wanted to discuss the situation with Dominic as soon as he was awake. They had fights from time to time, but soon made up. This altercation would be the same, she hoped.

By the time she had biscuits coming out of the oven, Dominic stood in the kitchen doorway. He looked incredibly sexy, with a day's growth of dark beard and a sleepy look around his eyes. He had changed, and the T-shirt he'd pulled on delineated every rock-hard muscle in his chest and shoulders. The jeans molded his lean physique. She turned away, wishing for the easy camaraderie they normally enjoyed. If it were another morning, she'd give him a kiss, and maybe suggest postponing breakfast while they detoured into the bedroom.

After their fight last night, she knew he'd refuse, and she was not into getting rebuffed.

"Breakfast is almost ready," she said, pointing to the coffeemaker.

"The smell of coffee woke me," he said. Crossing the small kitchen, he poured himself a cup.

As always, her heart gave a small skip when she saw him. He didn't say anything, just sipped the hot beverage and gazed out the window.

"How long are you going to be mad at me?" she asked finally, annoyed he was ignoring her.

There was silence for a moment. "This isn't like the other fights we've had, Annalise," he said, turning slowly to look at her. "You've rocked my world. I'm not sure if I will get over it."

That floored her. She leaned against the counter, unable to believe what he'd said, feeling a touch of panic.

"It changes my world, too, you know. We need to talk about this."

"There's nothing to discuss."

"There's lots to discuss," she said, clutching the edge of the counter tightly. "I know this wasn't the way we planned our life going, but it's not the end of the world."

"It may be the end of us," he said slowly.

Annalise felt as if he'd slapped her. She couldn't believe she'd heard him correctly.

"You do not mean that," she said hotly.

"I don't know what I mean. Talking isn't going to change anything, is it? I made my views known before we married. Nothing's changed for me. Seems as if we've reached a fork in the road."

"Once you get used to the idea, you'll feel better about it. You can talk to my father, or Tray or Mary Margaret's husband. You must know lots of men who are fathers. They'll all tell you it's a great thing. Not something bad."

"For them, not for me." He crossed to the table and pulled out a chair. Sitting, he studied the coffee in his mug.

She dished up the eggs, placed sausages on the side of each plate and carried them to the table. A moment later, she added the hot biscuits. Jam was already out. She poured some orange juice for each of them and then sat in her chair.

"So explain to me why having a baby is such a horrible thing," she said. If he'd only talk about it, maybe they could move beyond his anger.

"After breakfast," he said. He began to eat.

Annalise didn't have much appetite. She hated confrontation and disharmony. She'd rather clear the air and then eat, but maybe it was better this way. At least the food was hot.

They ate in silence. She studied him through the meal. He never once looked up, but kept his gaze focused on his plate of food. She thought about all the breakfasts they had shared over the years. When he was away, she missed their routine. In the early days of their marriage, she'd accompanied him on most of his assignments. As her own list of clients had grown she'd not been able to take off every time at a moment's notice. But she went often enough that they had seen a lot of the world together.

They would not forever be young, and on the fast track at work. She had reached a level that gave her a good income and still allowed her time for other pursuits. To her, stability and roots were important. She was grounded by her parents and grandparents, who had lived in the Washington metropolitan area all their lives. She wanted that grounding for her child. Travel was broadening, but staying home provided roots.

When he'd finished eating, Dominic rose and went for another cup of coffee. "Want any more?"

"No." She should cut out caffeine altogether, but couldn't yet forgo that first cup in the morning. The best she could do was limit her intake.

Clearing the dishes quickly, she ran water in the sink to let them soak. "Ready?"

He shrugged and leaned against the counter.

"Shouldn't we go and sit down or something?" she said.

"This won't take long. Before we were married we discussed having children. You came from a large family and said you were content with nieces and nephews. I was an only child with parents who had to get married and didn't really want a family."

Annalise nodded.

"They were young, and I don't know if they thought they loved each other or not. But my mother got pregnant and my dad did right by her—so he told her, over and over. And he didn't care in whose hearing he complained."

"It takes two," she murmured, wondering how a man could be so insensitive to a woman's feelings.

"Getting married and having a kid wasn't in my dad's plans—at least not at that point. He'd been raised in a mill town and had plans to escape. He wanted to move to New York, see about working in the theater—not as an actor, but behind the scenes. Instead, he was stuck in a small Pennsylvania town, with a wife and a kid and an old house that needed constant work. He ended up working in the mill."

"You told me that before."

"All his life he had to settle, because of one night that changed his world."

"You don't have to settle for anything," she protested. "For heaven's sake, Dominic, you can't compare that with us. You have a great career, and so do I. We don't have some shabby house. You don't have a dead-end job."

"I've seen what that kind of life is like. Men get bitter and turn old before their time. All focus is on the children—what they need, what their schedule is. Sacrifices have to be made so they'll have what they need. Soon it seems like the parents' lives revolve around the children. Look at your sister Mary Margaret—piano lessons, soccer practice, tutoring to get into the best schools. When do she and Sam have a life of their own?"

"My parents weren't like that."

"They still *are*, Annalise. When was the last time they went on a vacation that wasn't to the cottage? Have they ever been to Paris or Rome? Gone white-water rafting down the Colorado or skiing in Aspen?"

"They don't want to do that."

"Or there is no money and time to do that. Maybe they're just better at hiding their frustrations than my old man. He let it all hang out."

"We would not be like that, Dominic. You are nothing like your father. Circumstances are totally different. You make a great income. I have my own career, which has done well the last few years. We can afford to do what we want. We don't need to sacrifice things for the sake of tight financial circumstances."

He took a healthy drink of his coffee, tossing the remainder into the sink and putting his mug on the counter.

"What you don't know, and what I didn't tell you, is that I've been in this situation before," he said slowly. He hated talking about the past. But maybe it would help her understand.

She looked at him in confusion.

"What situation?"

"Expecting a baby."

Annalise stared. She couldn't believe what she'd heard. "You have a child somewhere?" There was a pause, then she jumped up. "We've known each other for more than six years. Been married five. And this is the first I'm hearing about it?" She looked stunned.

"No. I don't have a child. The baby was stillborn."

"Oh, how awful." That explained a lot, Annalise thought. He was afraid their child would be born dead.

"Our baby won't be born like that," she said gently, still reeling from the information. How could he have fathered another child and never told her? What of the baby's mother?

"You don't *know* how our baby will be born. Phyllis had a normal pregnancy. We thought everything was going along fine. But she went into labor two weeks early and the baby never drew a breath."

"Phyllis?" she repeated. The other woman had a name—of course. Annalise could hardly think.

"My wife. Ex-wife. First wife."

CHAPTER TWO

ANNALISE felt the blood pounding through her veins. Dominic was saying he'd had a wife before her. And she had never known a thing about it. He'd loved someone else. Fathered a child. And never mentioned a word. Would she have gone to her grave not knowing about that part of her husband's past if she hadn't become pregnant?

"You never told me you were married before," she said. She sat back down, wanting to weep. Then anger took hold. "How could you never tell me about such an important part of your past? I'm your *wife*. I haven't kept anything important from you. Where's the honesty needed in marriage? Don't you think that's something that should have been talked about at the onset? What happened?"

He paced across the room and back, frowning. "I never said anything because I've put it all behind me. I married Phyllis because it was the right thing to do—to give the baby a name and a father. I did it for her, too. We were high-school sweethearts. But I had plans to leave town and move on. For eight interminable months, I thought I was stuck, with no future except a life like my father's. When we didn't have the baby, we had nothing to hold us together. We divorced before I was twenty. I saved up and headed for college. My original plan, delayed a couple of years. You know I'm older than you, but that we graduated the same time. Now you know why."

"Married and divorced before you were twenty? Why not say something? You told me back then the reason you were late starting college was that you needed to work to save enough to attend," she said slowly, thinking back to those early days. Should she have picked up on some clue? How could he not have told her something this big in his past?

"That was true. All I had saved by my high-school graduation went to get Phyllis and me an apartment. For months, I thought I was doomed to repeat the life my father had—growing to resent the baby and Phyllis as I was stuck in some dead-end job in the mill town that was the one place I'd wanted to leave."

"Would you have?" she asked, caught up by the story, trying to picture a younger Dominic with some nebulous woman. She knew what the town looked like, but he didn't seem the type to be content there for his entire life.

"Probably."

"Probably not. You aren't your father. You set a goal and go for it. Look how fast you've gone up in the company. How much you know about all the various aspects of computer problems."

"It never came to the test," he said.

"Because the baby died?"

He nodded and turned to gaze out the window. He couldn't face her when he said, "And I've had to live with that guilt ever since."

Annalise frowned. "Why? You didn't cause its death. You said it was stillborn."

He ran his hand through his hair and shook his head.

"Intellectually, I know that. But it was a shock. My first reaction was relief—I could be free. Then I felt guilty for feeling that way. But Phyllis and I found we had little in common once we lived together. It was different when we were dating. The reality was unexpected. She was as glad as I was to get out of the marriage. I know you can't *think* a baby dead, but that's how I felt. That somehow my anger and resentment at not wanting the child caused its death. I should not have felt that way. What father doesn't want his child? My father excepted, of course. And then—me."

"So that's why you feel that way about our baby," she said, crossing her hands over her stomach in a protective manner. She had hardly gotten used to the idea, but already she felt she wanted to protect the growing life inside her.

"No! I do not wish this baby dead. I did not wish the other baby dead. I just wished for freedom. All I wanted then and now was to live life the way I planned. We have a great life. We entertain a wide group of friends. We take off on short notice to travel all over the world. Vacation wherever we wish, whenever we wish. We've built our life together. I don't want to lose it. To lose us."

"And that's what you fear if a baby's born?"

He closed his eyes. "I don't know," he said at last.

Annalise was reeling from the discovery that her husband had hidden a first marriage from her for as long as she'd known him. She'd thought they were a team. That it was the two of them against the world. Now she wasn't sure about anything anymore. What kind of marriage was based on secrets? She had been open about her past—not that she had anything of this proportion to reveal. Still, she expected honesty from her husband. Now his first marriage had come to light.

She'd known having a baby would change things, but she'd never considered this. "What other secrets do you have?" she asked.

He looked at her, anguish in his expression. "I should have told you. But it never seemed the right time. And then it just wasn't important. We moved here, got our careers going, and I moved on."

"So fear of not being able to do whatever you wish keeps you from wanting children?"

"That makes it sound cold and selfish. Maybe it is. But I've seen what having a child does to people. I know how my father was. That's the kind of parenting I know. I don't want to be like that."

"Lots of families have children. The parents are happy. The children enrich their lives. You do not have to be like your father."

"And children keep other people in dead-end jobs, living from paycheck to paycheck with nothing to look forward to. Kids get them caught up in the treadmill of dreary routine, substandard housing, losing hope for any kind of a different future."

"But that's not you or me. We're young, we have good jobs, and so far, we have done all we wanted to do." She tried to reason with Dominic again, to get him to understand that their future would be different.

She rubbed her stomach slowly. She felt sad for a baby whose parents weren't deliriously happy at its coming. She hoped this baby knew nothing of what was going on.

He frowned, following the movement of her hand for a moment. "Maybe thought waves are more powerful than people think. I wished a hundred times or more that Phyllis had not gotten pregnant. Then the baby was born dead."

"It's sad. But you can't think an outcome like that. Even if Phyllis had thought that, it wouldn't have resulted in a stillborn baby."

"I'll never get over the guilt," he said softly.

He looked out the window again. "I've been called about another assignment—this time to Hong Kong. It'll give us a chance to think things over."

"Think what over? Whether you want it or not, we're going to be parents. No matter what you think or say now, you are going to be a father. I guess it's up to you to decide exactly what kind of father you'll be!"

She turned and walked to the bedroom. She didn't know whether to cry or smash something. She grabbed her tote and packed a couple of outfits and sleepwear. She was going to Lianne's. Her twin would give her some advice and comfort. How could Dominic have kept his first marriage secret? She felt a pang at the thought of him being another woman's husband. Living a life she'd never even known about. They'd had an apartment together. Made a baby together. Tears threatened. Damn, he should have told her before they married about his past.

What had the other woman been like? Had the loss of their baby been so great neither could get over it? *He'd made a baby with someone else.* The thought caused a new twist of pain.

She was not going to lose *her* baby. Maybe she hadn't wanted one to begin with, but the idea was growing. She'd have another grandchild for her parents. She and her twin would have babies the same age. Maybe they wouldn't be as close as she and Lianne were, but they'd be first cousins, sharing a lot.

How could Dominic be so pigheaded as not to even consider changing his attitude when she was expecting a child? She would love this baby if only because it was part of Dominic. He could wish it away as much as he wanted. Fear of being a father was no excuse. *She'd* never been a mother before. She'd do the best she could and hope it was enough. That was all any parent could do.

She went to the front door. Dominic was leaning against the doorjamb to the kitchen, watching her without saying a word.

"I'm going to Lianne's."

"I'll be leaving soon. I'll call you from Hong Kong."

She wanted to make a grand exit and say something scathing like, *Don't bother.* But she was afraid if she opened her mouth she'd burst into tears. Staring at him, she saw a phantom woman hovering beside him. Someone else who had kissed him, slept with him. Had a baby with him. The hurt was overwhelming.

She shook her head and left.

Blinking back tears, she made the drive to Lianne and Tray's condo in record time. She sat in the car for a moment, trying to gain control. She left the tote in the car. If Dominic was leaving, she could return home later. But first she wanted to see her sister.

When Lianne opened the door, Annalise tried to smile, but she burst into tears instead.

"What's wrong?" Lianne asked, hugging her sister. "Whatever has happened?"

"Dominic doesn't want the baby," Annalise wailed.

"My baby?" Lianne asked.

"No—ours."

Dominic finished packing and headed for the living room. He'd pack his laptop and then be ready to leave. The routine was established; he could do it without thinking.

He had seen the stunned hurt in Annalise's eyes when he'd told her of his first marriage. The image haunted him. All these years, he'd thought he'd put that so far behind him it would never rise up again. Now it was out for all to see, and his guilt had not diminished one iota. How could any man wish away a baby? Wasn't that telling enough? Who could want to be around a person like that? He was just like his old man. Worse. And he hated the idea.

No matter how hard anyone worked, they never escaped the past. Now events were repeating themselves. His wife was expecting a baby, and it was the last thing he'd ever thought they'd have.

His father had been a bitter old man long before his time. Dominic remembered his mother had tried hard to please him, but nothing she'd done had succeeded. Dominic had loved his mother, but he felt sad thinking of all she'd missed out of life by having a baby so young, and then living with a resentful man who complained about their circumstances.

Dominic had worked hard to make a different life for himself. At the cost of his lost baby. He rubbed his hands across his face. When they had returned from the baby's brief funeral service, Phyllis had told him she didn't want to stay married. It had saved him asking her for a divorce. Once again he'd felt the taste of freedom—and the guilt at having things turn out that way. Even now, more than ten years later, he could feel the gnawing guilt.

Time to shove those memories away. He had a plane to catch. He wished he could have changed things for Annalise. But he was only human, and the thought of a baby scared him to death. Maybe he'd think differently once the idea seeped in. But for now, he wanted out.

Even out of his marriage? He'd almost implied that. Did he mean it?

Marriage to Annalise had proved to be a wondrous thing. They liked the same foods and restaurants. She enjoyed the theater, symphony and traveling—all new to him when he'd come to Washington for college. They had so much in common—from books and movies to their tastes in furnishings. He looked around the living room, remembering the purchase of every item. Nothing like the floral prints her mother had throughout the O'Mallory family home. Their place was sleek and modern—like Annalise herself.

Having a baby—even being pregnant—would change her. Phyllis had been fun enough when they'd been dating. But, once pregnant, her entire existence had revolved around that state. He couldn't go through that again. Couldn't bear to see Annalise change before his eyes.

He couldn't believe the past was repeating itself.

Lianne pulled Annalise over to the sofa.

Tray came out from the back of the flat. "Annalise— I didn't know you were coming over," he said. Taking a closer look, he raised his eyebrows in silent question to his wife.

"We're having a bit of a crisis. Be a love and find something to do," Lianne said.

"Right. Think I have something to do at the office." Tray bade them goodbye and left.

"Astute man," Annalise said, blotting her eyes with the tissue her twin had provided, wishing her husband had been as astute. She was mixed up about this pregnancy, and she needed his support, not to be stunned by news of his past.

"He's wonderful. But you've always thought Dominic was, as well," Lianne said, rubbing her back.

"Before today," Annalise said. "Or last night. He was horrid when I said I was pregnant."

"And you're just now telling *me!*" Lianne exclaimed. "That's great news. I'm thrilled for you both!"

"Don't be." Annalise explained everything. "He's still in shock over the news. But he will come back," she ended. "Don't you think?"

"Of course he will. You two make a great team. And the news takes a while to process. But I can't believe he was married before and never told you. I'm more than a bit surprised by that," Lianne said.

"*You* are? Imagine how *I* feel. All this time, I thought I knew the man, and now he springs this on me. Why not before we were married? Why not the first time he met me? He could have said something like *I'm just back in the dating game from a divorce.*"

"What did he say? What reasons did he give for not telling you before?"

"I didn't ask. I was too surprised by it all. Darn it, it makes me so angry to think he kept something this important a secret. What does that say about our relationship?"

Lianne thought for a moment. "I think once he realizes what he sounds like, he'll be back so fast your head will spin. Nothing is like it was all those years ago. He's crazy about you. The two of you always seemed as if you were in a world of your own—outsiders beware."

Annalise shook her head. "Not anymore. I don't know how to get over this. I feel as if he's a complete stranger. We've lived together for five years, and never once did it come up. He deliberately kept it from me."

"It's early yet. Give yourself some time. And you've got to try and think of it from Dominic's point of view."

"Which I already know."

"Not necessarily. He was unhappy in that marriage, that's for sure. Maybe he wanted to be a carefree college kid like everyone else. There probably weren't too many twenty-year-old college students who already had a divorce behind them. I could see him not spreading *that* around," Lianne said thoughtfully.

"He wouldn't have been spreading it around to tell *me*—especially when we began to discuss marriage."

"I don't know. What you had together sounds so fresh and free—unlike his first marriage. I could see him wanting to pretend life was as it *was,* not as it had been."

"Maybe." Could Lianne be right?

"Ask him. I bet he says he wanted to forget the past and forge a new life."

"Which he did. But now circumstances are similar, and he's freaked. I didn't expect to get pregnant. I sure didn't plan on it. He's blaming me."

Lianne shrugged. "Do you realize we are pregnant together? Good grief, sis—everyone will think it's because we're twins."

"Maybe it is. Maybe I felt your longing. The birth control failed. Who knows why now, after five years of marriage, the method failed? Dominic asked if it were a twin thing."

"So now it's *my* fault?" Lianne asked with a twinkle.

"No fault. I'm going to have a baby!" Annalise said. Slowly she began to smile. "A part of me and Dominic. How could anyone not be happy about that?"

"Dominic needs to talk to Tray. That man is so delighted you'd think we invented the concept of children."

"I'm happy for you. What should I do?" Annalise said slowly.

Lianne looked at her sister closely. "What do you want to do?"

"Make Dominic as happy about this as I'm becoming. Pretend I never heard of his first wife. Make everything come out happy."

"And if you can't?"

"What can I do? I'm pregnant. That's not going to change—at least for nine months. It was a shock to me when I first realized it, but now I'm growing to love this baby. I'll have to go on, I guess." She said the words, but she couldn't really believe them. Dominic wouldn't end their marriage over this. Even if he did, he'd still be a father to their child. Had he thought of that?

"Go on?" Lianne asked.

"I make a good living. I could support myself and the baby."

"I don't mean that. I mean, what plans are you making—contingency plans in case he doesn't come around—to change his mind?"

Annalise lay back against the cushions, resting her head and looking up at the ceiling.

"I don't have any. I'm relying on his good sense."

Lianne sighed. "Sometimes people don't have good sense. Especially if they have some phobia from the past."

"So how do I combat something like that?" Annalise asked. "He needs to come to the realization that this is not the same." She didn't tell her sister the rest—how he'd felt relieved, then guilty, when his first baby had not lived. There were some things too sacred to be shared outside of their marriage.

"So you and the baby would just live with him and hope he comes around?" Lianne asked.

"Not exactly. Perhaps I need to put myself first. I can't afford to wait for Dominic to come around. Maybe I could look into buying a home to live in with the baby. One was listed a while ago with our office which has loads of potential. It reminds me of Grandma Carrie and Grandpa Paul's home. It would require a load of work to bring it up to the kind of place I envision." She looked at her sister. "I don't see the apartment as a baby's home. I'll need different furnishings, a place for a stroller and later a bike. And a yard for a kid to run around in."

"We're planning to raise our child in *this* flat," Lianne said.

"I know, but somehow I want a more traditional home for my baby. I haven't had a lot of time to think it through, but I'd love to have a place like we had growing up—complete with yard and friendly neighbors. Anyway, I'll have to think about it some more."

"If you find a home, buy it. It'll give you something to think about besides Dominic. He has to make his decision for himself. You have to make yours. I hope they coincide, but if not, you have a life to live," Lianne said.

"I want to live it with Dominic. Perhaps if he sees how serious I am about our future—all of our futures—together, he'll want to be a part of it."

"You have your baby to think about now. Whatever happens, I'm in your corner."

When Annalise left her sister's after lunch, she drove by the home she'd mentioned to Lianne. She'd seen it on a home tour months ago. Now, stopping in front, she could see it definitely needed a lot of work. The yard was a mess; the house needed paint. But it had good bones and the lot was spacious. She could imagine children running on the lawn, playing tag or catch. Maybe they'd even get a small dog.

Whoa—she hadn't even convinced her husband to be happy about the baby, and now she was envisioning them all living happily ever after in this run-down house?

Dominic would probably freak when he saw it. She'd never seen his childhood home in Pennsylvania. His father had lived in an apartment by the time she'd met him. But she'd have to make this a showplace to convince him it was a wise move. *If* she decided to do it.

Feeling marginally better with the idea, when Annalise reached home, she went to the den to pull out the listing for the house. She spent some moments calculating the figures. With luck, she could swing the purchase of the house herself—without Dominic's support. It wouldn't leave much money to renovate with, but she'd do what she could as the money came. She'd just have to sell a few more higher-end homes.

Dominic had been right. The baby would bring changes. But change wasn't necessarily bad. The apartment suited their current lifestyle. A cozy family home would suit their future lifestyle.

Later that evening, she pampered herself with a long soak in a hot tub, then went to bed early with a good book. But she couldn't read. It was the first time since she'd left Lianne's that she'd let herself think about Dominic's past, and she couldn't let it go. She tried to imagine him as a husband to another woman—with a totally different life. But their life kept imposing itself. The parties they'd given, which they'd both enjoyed so much. The boating trips they shared in summer came to mind. What about skiing in Aspen? An annual event she took for granted. And the week they'd spent in Switzerland one winter had special memories. She couldn't imagine life being different.

Her mother and grandmothers had stayed home with their children. Was that the right way to raise kids? How could she give up the work she loved? Maybe she would cut back, but she couldn't imagine staying home with a baby all the time. Beside, once the child grew and was in school, she'd be bored staying home with nothing to do.

Had Phyllis planned to stay home with their baby? What had she wanted for her life before she got pregnant? Maybe Dominic hadn't been the only one whose dreams shattered. Had he considered Phyllis at all?

She admitted to herself that she was incredibly hurt that Dominic had not confided in her before. Did that show a fundamental lack of trust and commitment in their marriage? Was she good enough to be part of a fun-loving couple, but not for the intimate details of life?

That made her angry. She fed that anger when she thought of Dominic's reaction to the news about their baby. It had been just as much a shock to her as to him, darn it. Where was his concern for her? Didn't he consider she was going through some major readjustments herself?

The next five days passed slowly. Dominic called when he reached Hong Kong. With the twelve-hour time difference, it was hard to coordinate calling times convenient to both after that. She called him on Wednesday, but reached his voice mail. He had not returned that call.

She tried to keep busy, but more and more she ended up thinking about the revelation he'd made, and how that might impact their lives. Her anger simmered each day. She was unable to have it all out with Dominic, and yet unable to let it go.

Annalise plunged into working, determined to find each client the perfect home for them. And she toyed with the idea of buying that house. Lianne urged her onward. Annalise had driven by the house each day, and by Friday, had made up her mind. She'd buy the place and hoped things worked out the way she planned.

Annalise was able to get very good financing, due to her connections in the real-estate community. Offering a much lower price than the asking price, due to the work needing to be done and the length of time the place had already been on the market, she was delighted when the owners accepted. The house was tied up in probate, and her purchase would enable it to move along the process that much faster.

The attorneys agreed to a rent-purchase agreement that allowed Annalise access to the house immediately. She couldn't wait to get started on renovations. Better to do them as soon as possible, before she became too limited by pregnancy.

With any luck, she would have all the renovations finished by the time the baby was born.

Everything would go more quickly if Dominic helped. He'd worked his way through college in construction, and he was much more knowledgeable about such things than Annalise, even though she'd been helping her father and brothers all her life.

Of course she'd ask for volunteers from her family. With that crew aboard, she'd probably have everything completed easily in no time. But she wanted the project to be hers and Dominic's. Maybe having a joint goal would get them back on track as a couple.

The days seemed endless without him. She vacillated between anger and regret that so much had changed. Uncertainty plagued her. He hadn't really suggested they consider separating. She'd interjected that idea herself, and it was one she hated.

The following Friday, she picked up the keys to her new place and stopped off after work. It was a sunny fall day, but colder than normal, and she could feel the chill in the old house. She'd called the local power company and arranged to have the power turned on. Tomorrow, when she came to begin work, she'd turn on the heat. But for today, she just wanted to wander through, decide what she wanted to do in each room and make a short list of priority tasks.

It was after eight when she arrived back at the flat. There was a message on the answering machine from Dominic. Had he deliberately called when she was not home to avoid talking with her? She checked the time. On other Fridays she *would* have been home at that time. She hated that she'd missed him. Dialing the number he'd left, she reached the hotel in Hong Kong. But he had already gone out for the day.

Taking one of the pregnancy books she'd borrowed from Lianne, she curled up on the sofa and began to read. Before ten, she fell asleep.

Waking in the morning, she had a crick in her neck and did not feel fully rested. But excitement about the new house had her rising quickly to get ready for the day.

She'd just come from the shower when the phone rang. Dashing out to get it, wrapped in her warm robe, she recognized Dominic's voice immediately.

"Hi," she said breathlessly. "Your timing's good. I just got out of the shower. It's almost dinner time there, right?"

"Yeah. I called to say I'm leaving Hong Kong tomorrow and heading straight for San Francisco."

"Coming home through San Francisco?"

"Not yet. There's a project there that needs some work. I might also swing up through Seattle and check on a couple of clients there, since I'll be on the West Coast."

Annalise sat on the arm of the sofa. "So when will you be home?" she asked, anger flaring that she was still to be denied their discussion. It was not one she wanted to have over the phone.

"You know how it goes. My job takes me everywhere. Sometimes for a day or two, sometimes for longer."

"But generally you have a break between assignments," she said evenly. She would not allow her frustration to show. He was deliberately staying away. But he couldn't live out of his suitcase forever.

"I'll call you from San Francisco."

"Maybe I should fly out to join you."

"No."

Nothing more. She swallowed hard and bit her lower lip. The rejection hurt. Any other time *he* would have suggested she join him. She didn't like this rift between them.

"Okay. I won't. Take care." She put the receiver back in place and congratulated herself for not slamming it down. *Do your own thing and I'll do mine,* she thought in defiance as she went to get dressed. She had not mentioned the house. Of course he'd be surprised—but not as surprised as she'd been to learn of his marriage.

The thought still made her angry! She wasn't sure exactly which was worse—to learn he had been married before, or not to have been told earlier in their relationship.

What would she do if he truly didn't get over her pregnancy and left her?

She refused to even think about that. She had work to do today, and was glad for the distraction.

Arriving at the house some time later, Annalise turned on the heat and carried her broom, mop, bucket and cleaning supplies into the kitchen. That would be the first room she tackled. She had the vacuum cleaner in the car, and would bring more items with every trip. She had enough cleaning to last for days. Once the previous owner had died, her out-of-town heirs had not kept the place up.

There was a definite satisfaction in washing down the cupboards and counters and knowing the home would be hers for many years. She wondered if she was getting the nesting instinct from being pregnant—or was it just the next logical step in the maturing process? The apartment had been a great first home. But this was a house that would welcome a family through all its stages, from new babies through grandparenting.

Had Dominic and Phyllis rented a house or an apartment? Had they made plans for naming the baby, for raising a child? Had they ever thought about being grandparents?

Stop that, she admonished herself. She had gotten into the habit of questioning everything—trying to envision how that earlier pregnancy had been. She needed answers to her curiosity so she could stop dwelling on the past. It was like touching an aching tooth—it hurt, but she couldn't stop. She needed to know all the details and hope she could then put it behind her and move on.

She took a quick break for lunch, and then swung by a hardware store to gather some paint samples to take back with her. Dominic's favorite color was yellow, and that would be a perfect sunny color for the kitchen.

She'd have one of her brothers help her paint the room. She didn't relish climbing on ladders or stools to reach the high part of the walls. She was taking no chances with this precious baby she carried.

The weekend flew by. Annalise was tired Monday morning, but headed off to work, already counting the hours until she could be back at the house.

Dominic exited the jetway and merged with the other travelers heading for Customs at San Francisco International Airport on Monday morning. He was tired. Changing time zones had an effect, but his fatigue was due more to lack of sleep than to his flight back to the States. How long would he wrestle with what to do? He needed to make a decision and stick with it.

Was he less noble this time around? He'd thought marriage the best thing to do when Phyllis had gotten pregnant. The baby had been his; he'd lived up to his re-sponsibilities. And he'd done his best to be a good hus-band. The affection he'd felt for her had faded with the day-to-day hardships of life, but he'd always done what he thought right. Just like his father. Only he hadn't voiced his frustrations and disappointments to Phyllis. She'd had it hard enough without listening to his complaints.

This time he was already married, and his wife was expecting his baby. He should accept his duty and be there for Annalise.

Only, the circumstances were different. Phyllis had not had a high-paying job, nor a large family to offer moral support. She'd been in her teens. He'd been young, too. They'd learned a lot during the months they'd lived together. He'd never forget that year. The ups and downs and the ending.

He had never held the baby, only seen it at a distance. Since they had not decided on a name prior to her birth, she'd quickly been given his mother's— Susan—to have something to put on the tombstone. They should have taken more time to decide on a name. Once he'd left the cemetery, that bleak winter's day, he'd never been back.

What if Annalise had problems during pregnancy? He clenched his teeth. He couldn't deal with the pain and guilt a second time.

Dominic moved up in the queue, and was soon through Customs and on his way to the downtown area of San Francisco. He was tired of thinking about duty and regrets and lost opportunities. He had just left one of the world's most exciting cities and was entering another. Next week, who knew? This was the life he had craved as a teenager. The goal he'd set for himself all those years of working his way through college and honing his skills. Learning all he could, applying that knowledge and finding a job that would combine each aspect.

If he gave it up, would he turn out like his old man? Bitter, grumpy, and stuck in one place the rest of his life?

Not according to Annalise. But she'd slant things to go *her* way. He needed to get a clear view of the situation. Not be swayed by pretty blue eyes.

Two weeks of thinking still had not given him a clear-cut direction.

In the meantime, he missed Annalise.

After checking into his hotel and calling the office, he took off. San Francisco was a great city for walking. Compacted into a small space, the various neighborhoods could be reached in a short time.

Every time he thought about the coming baby, he felt

hemmed in, and he needed to get out where he felt no walls were closing in.

The air was cool blowing off the Bay. He remembered the last time he and Annalise had visited San Francisco. They had taken a few days to explore the city, from Chinatown to Golden Gate Park to the financial district. Though summer, the weather had been cool, with a sea fog that blanketed the city each morning. Today's temperatures were also cool, but he was alone. No Annalise to find enchantment in everything she saw.

Today, nothing held his interest.

Dominic walked along the wharf, looking at the sidewalk cafés, remembering how much Annalise had enjoyed eating fresh crab from the sidewalk vendors as they walked along. He continued toward Pier 39, the huge converted pier that housed stores, shops, restaurants and loads of tourist attractions. Schlocky, he'd thought. She had loved every inch. Consequently, he'd gone in almost every shop and caught some of her enthusiasm.

Stopping at a bench on the grassy area before the pier, he sat and idly watched the other people—families for the most part. For a moment, he wondered why these children weren't in school on an October Monday, but he figured they were all tourists, taking advantage of a quiet season. Children ran around laughing with glee; mothers chased after them. One man was trying to help his little boy fly a kite. The wind was strong enough, but the boy kept trying to run after the kite, rather then let it soar.

Dominic wondered what was going through the father's mind. He seemed to be having a good time, if his laughter was an indicator. For a long moment, Dominic watched. That little boy was going to have some wonderful memories. Having fun, sharing their day together.

He remembered picnics his mother had taken him on when he'd been little. Those were happy memories. He didn't remember his father being part of them.

Intellectually, he knew many families were happy together. He'd witnessed Annalise's own family enough over the years. Patrick and Helen O'Mallory never seemed to resent having so many children. Would he and Phyllis have worked things out, found some contentment in their lives, if their baby had lived?

In retrospect, he doubted it. They had not drawn closer with the impending birth of their baby. And once they'd no longer had that tie, they'd had nothing to say to each other.

Some people were obviously wired differently. He wasn't father material.

He stood and began walking again. Watching families only made him feel more lonely. If he decided not to be part of Annalise's life, he could do exactly as he wished—but alone. Would that be better than resenting the ties a child presented?

CHAPTER THREE

ANNALISE packed a small suitcase with an assortment of clothing. She included several outfits for work. The majority of the other items she placed in were clothes like jeans and shirts, that could be tossed in the washer after a hard day's cleaning. She collected a few more items and headed out. She'd had enough of going to work, then home and the house. There was no one to be home for. She might as well save travel time and live at the house.

Her brother Sean had moved the bed from her second bedroom to the house for her last night. He'd been the first in the family to see the place, and had thought she was crazy to try to fix it up.

Maybe she *had* taken on more than originally estimated, but the house was growing on her. Each room she cleaned, and planned to renovate, seemed to reaffirm her decision. She wanted to bring it to life again. Hear children laughing and running down the steps. Savor the memories they'd make at holidays and birthdays. Make her mark on every inch of the place.

She'd suggested Sean might wish to help, as well, but he'd quickly given her several reasons why he couldn't.

Not that her brother was the handiest man around. He preferred to hire help if he needed anything done.

Once she'd put her things away in the small closet in the bedroom she'd chosen, Annalise sat on the bed and glanced around. She had wanted to paint the kitchen first, but maybe she needed a happy place to stay the night, as well. The faded wallpaper on these walls needed quick removal. For a moment, the tasks facing her were daunting. She hardly knew where to begin.

Dominic would know exactly what to do to bring the house to life. The best *she* could do was to learn as she went. And daydream about what it could be instead of what it was.

By Friday, Annalise had moved more items into the house—two chairs and a small table to eat at. The television from the apartment guestroom was set up in her bedroom. Bathroom items, extra towels and sheets were essential. Enough pots and pans and dishes to keep her going. She hated to return to the apartment. It echoed with emptiness, and she couldn't forget for a moment Dominic's reaction to her news, or the surprising revelation that had rocked her.

"Don't worry, baby," she said, rubbing her still-flat tummy. "We'll be fine."

One way or another, including the time before they married, when they'd already been a couple, they'd been more than six years together. Now Annalise felt cut loose, on her own. She'd stay awake nights worrying over the future—could Dominic have really meant what he said about the end of their marriage?

She vacillated between determination to make this marriage work and writing off the man she felt she had never fully known. How dare he carelessly throw away five years of marriage? Even suggest it! What about the bond between them? What about love?

It was not a word they used frequently. She loved Dominic. She'd thought he loved her. Her family easily hugged and kissed when seeing each other. Dominic came from a background where that was unknown. She'd recognized that early on, and had gradually, over their years together, come to accept the affections he bestowed as the best he could do.

It had nothing to do with their time making love. He was an ardent lover. She missed the passion in their marriage more and more as the days went by. He had rarely been gone as long as this trip—unless he'd taken her with him.

This time apart gave her an idea of what life without him would be like. And she didn't like it.

Was Dominic returning?

She had not telephoned him since he'd arrived in San Francisco. When he got back, he'd figure out where to find her. He had her cell phone number. That was all he'd need.

Saturday, Lianne and Tray stopped by before leaving for Richmond. Tray's uncle had left him a house and they were fixing it up to sell. It was the first time they had seen Annalise's purchase. Lianne walked through the rooms of the house and said at the end of the tour that she was glad they had far less to do to get their home ready than Annalise did.

"I can put my own design ideas on it," Annalise said defensively. She was still feeling a tiny bit over-whelmed. She wanted her sister to approve. She wanted backing for the coming confrontation with her husband.

If they were to continue, she'd definitely need his help with renovations.

"There are easier ways to make your mark," Lianne said with twinly candor. "In addition to getting the house habitable, the yard looks as if it'll take forever to make it useable. Maybe you could rent it out as some horror-movie set."

"Very funny. I can learn about gardening." She didn't have to have everything fixed up in the first six months. But Lianne had a point. The yard was a disaster—nothing like the groomed lawn she could envision her baby playing on.

"Dominic will be a help with the major renovation," Tray said as he stood on the back porch, surveying the overgrown tangle of plants and shrubs. "He'll probably need a chainsaw out here, though."

Annalise kept quiet. Until she knew exactly what Dominic's plans were, she was keeping silent around her family. Only Lianne knew of any problem Annalise wanted to keep it that way.

"Is Dominic still in Hong Kong?" Lianne asked. She shivered slightly in the cold and they returned to the old kitchen.

"He's on the west coast now, checking in with clients in San Francisco and then Seattle."

"I thought they'd bring him right home," Tray said. "He's been gone a lot lately, hasn't he?"

"I think they are on an economy kick, and want to have him stop by as many clients as possible on the way back from Asia," Annalise said, making it up as she went. She didn't want to discuss Dominic until she knew more.

Lianne studied her sister for a moment. For a second Annalise thought she was going to ask an embarrassing question about what she knew about Dominic's plans. But her sister merely raised her eyebrows and then looked away. Tray apparently knew nothing about what she'd told Lianne, and she was grateful her sister hadn't shared.

They left soon thereafter, to drive to Richmond. Annalise felt lonely after their visit. They had been full of plans for updating Tray's house, decorating it to help sell it quickly. Annalise wanted that kind of planning with Dominic. Discussing ideas, selecting colors and furnishings—as they had when decorating their flat.

Instead, he didn't even know about the house. And, after his reaction to her pregnancy announcement, she was worried how he'd react.

But a child needed a house. She had had several comfortable places growing up—the large home her parents owned, those of her grandparents and the huge house by the sea, misnamed the cottage. She wanted the same for her child.

By midafternoon Annalise was exhausted. She had not been plagued with morning sickness, but she certainly didn't have the stamina she normally had. A nap every afternoon was coming to be the norm for her to be able to keep going. She lay down on her bed, and in no time was sound asleep.

Her cell phone woke her a short time later.

"Did we get robbed?" Dominic's voice asked.

"Where are you? Home?" She was groggy from her nap. She sat up on the edge of the mattress, trying to wake up.

"Yes. The bed is gone from the second room, and the television. What else is missing?"

"Cleaning supplies, some clothes. The card table and chairs. It saves travel time if I stay here while you're gone."

"And where exactly *is* 'here'?"

Annalise took a deep breath. "At the house I bought."

Dominic uttered an epithet. "What house?"

"I was going to talk to you about it, but you've been gone a while."

"Less than three weeks. And in that time you bought a house without mentioning it to me?"

"It's perfect for children. It has a large yard, it's in a quiet neighborhood and a good school district. We had the listing, so I took advantage of a great price and bought it."

"Seems you've decided how you want your life to go. Have a good one." He hung up.

"Dominic—" She was talking to dead air.

She couldn't have handled it any worse, she thought, lying back down. She closed her eyes and thought of a dozen things she should have said. It seemed as if the only way she knew how make major announcements was to blurt them out. She needed to go to the flat and explain.

Only, she was so tired. She'd had to set her alarm so she wouldn't sleep through the appointment she had at six. A couple was flying in from New York, and Annalise had lined up two homes for them to view.

She opened one eye to check the time. Not enough to dash home and see Dominic. Not and have the discussion they needed. She'd take the time to rest up, then have a quick shower before meeting her appointment at the office. She'd get home late, but at least she knew he'd be there, and they could talk as long as they wanted.

It was after ten when Annalise returned to the flat. She had another sale to her credit. Her clients had loved the first house, seen the second, and then returned to the first for another walk-through. Annalise had been amazed at how fast the sale had gone. It was a real estate agent's dream—full list price and financing already approved.

All she thought about on the way back to the flat was that she would be able to use her commission for some of the needed repairs around her house.

"Hello?" she called as she shut the front door behind her. The apartment was dark. Only a light from the den shed any illumination. She couldn't help comparing Dominic's arrival this time with his last one. Then he hadn't been able to wait to sweep her into bed. This trip had produced an unsatisfactory phone call that he had ended abruptly.

"I'm in the office," he replied.

He sat at the computer and hardly looked up when she entered.

"Hi—glad you're home," she said, leaning over to kiss him. He turned his face so the kiss landed on his cheek.

Apparently things had not improved with time to think things through, she thought wryly. He wasn't the only one to have to think. She'd come up with some ideas herself.

"Home for long?" she asked, slipping out of her jacket and tossing it across a chair.

"Until the next assignment," he said. "I didn't expect to see you. I thought you were ensconced at your house. The one I didn't even know about."

"If you were home more, maybe you'd know. Or perhaps if you called once in a while."

"I did call. You were out. At the house?"

"It needs work before we can move in. I was just

staying there while you were gone to save travel time and squeeze some work in during the evenings, rather than run back and forth all the time. At least it gave me something to do while you were away. I'll come home, of course, now that you're back."

He looked at her, then glanced around the den. "I have no plans to move in. This is my home."

Annalise shook her head. "You haven't seen it yet. It needs renovation, but it would suit a family much better than a high-rise apartment."

His expression tightened. "I haven't even gotten used to the idea of there being a baby and now you're talking about changing everything—like our very home."

"You weren't here to discuss this with."

"You knew I was coming back. What's the rush?"

"Someone else might have bought the house." It was unlikely, but Dominic wasn't to know that. "Besides, I needed something else to think about than the fact my husband had a whole other family he never told me about," she said.

Dominic didn't say a word, but leaned back in the desk chair. His gaze roved over her figure, stopping momentarily at her waist. She was not showing. It was too soon for that. What would he think when she was fat and waddling?

He turned back to the computer.

She wanted to smack him. They were having the most important crisis of their marriage and he was ignoring it for work.

She walked over to the desk and pulled a notepad closer, writing down the address.

"That's where I'll be," she said, tossing it into the center of the desk.

He swung around and looked at her. "You're living there for good?"

"I was just staying there until you came back, but if you are going to ignore me, I might as well stay for good. I thought we could talk when you got home."

"What do you want to talk about?"

"Gee—nothing like that comment to kill conversation. I don't know. How was San Francisco? Was it raining in Seattle? Want to come see the house?"

He rubbed his hands over his face, then stood. "I've thought about the situation nonstop all the time I was gone. I can't help how I feel, Annalise."

"Feelings and actions are two different things," she shot back.

"I understand that. I have not acted on my feelings."

"Which are?"

"Frustration, anger. Dammit, I thought I had my life on track. You've derailed it."

She put her fists on her hips. "Not me, *we!* I did not get pregnant alone."

"Neither did Phyllis."

Feeling instantly deflated, she leaned against the edge of the desk. She hated being categorized with his first wife.

"Did she deliberately become pregnant to keep you there?" she asked. She wanted to know every detail.

"I accused her of that. She denied it. I've always had my doubts."

"You said *she* asked for the divorce."

"The reality of the months we were married was far different than any fantasy of marriage. She was no more interested in continuing the relationship than I was."

"What if the baby had lived, grown up?"

Dominic thought about it for a moment. "She would have been nine now. What grade is that?"

"Third, I think," Annalise said.

"Hard to imagine."

"But if she had lived, would you still be married to Phyllis?"

He looked at her and shrugged. "Who knows? I wanted out. She was reasonably content to live there."

"But we never would have met. Would that be a good thing or bad?" she mused.

"Can you imagine the last six years not knowing each other?" he asked.

She stared at him as she thought through the question. Her life would have been totally different. Would she have been as happy?

"Do you love me, Dominic?"

He stuffed his hands into his pockets, returning her gaze. "Would we be married if I did not?"

"Probably. We're good together—in bed and out. We have similar likes and dislikes. We have a lot in common, yet enough differences to keep things interesting. Do you love me?" she asked again.

"Is this a trick question? If I loved you, I'd love your baby?" he asked.

"No, but that's not a bad thought. This baby is part of you, and I'm thrilled we are having a child to be part of *us*. I thought we had a strong marriage. Now I'm not so sure. What are you going to do about this child? Whether you live with us or apart, you are the baby's father, and you will have to deal with that."

"I don't know if I can," he said.

She wanted to shake him. If she could be a mother, he could be a father.

"You do have a few months to get used to the idea," she said dryly. Turning, she went to the door. "Call me when you want to talk," she said.

"Wait."

She turned, hope blossoming instantly.

He sighed slightly and inclined his head. "Tell me about this house you bought."

As an olive branch, it wasn't much. But she'd take it.

"The sale is still pending. I qualified for the loan on my own earnings and then obtained a rent-to-purchase deal so I could take it on immediately. All the inspections are complete, and the appraisal went through. But I wanted to get started on renovations since I have a time limit."

He nodded. But Annalise wasn't sure he was listening. He looked at her, but she wondered if he really saw her.

Or was it Phyllis he saw? Was it Phyllis he was fighting against? She wished she knew for certain.

"I've started cleaning every room. And making a list of all I can do and what I need to have others help with. I think I'd like to hire a construction worker part-time. If I can manage the expense. My commission on today's sale will help. I'm trying to get enough business four days a week to enable me to take an extra day at the weekend for more concentrated time to tackle the various projects." She'd hoped he'd offer to help.

"I thought you'd enlist the aid of your family."

"I asked Sean. He sounded horrified. Lianne and Tray are working on getting the house Tray inherited from his uncle ready for sale. And they've already asked some of my other brothers, so I'll have to wait in line. There are only so many weekends. Once their place is done, maybe the boys'll help me out."

"I'm sure they will."

Annalise hated the way the conversation was going. She had more enthusiastic responses from her co-workers. Dominic was not offering any help.

"You've been gone for days, and this is the best you can do?" she asked.

He stared at her for a moment, then shrugged.

"Fine." She turned and headed for the front door. He crossed after her to stop her.

"I need some more time," Dominic said.

"It's not going to change anything. The baby will still be born when it's due. The doctor said early June. I'm trying to get a family home ready. Come see the house. It's a bit of a mess right now, but with some renovations it'll be wonderful." She outlined some of her ideas.

"What you describe is a boat-load of work to make it habitable. The house is eighty years old. You'll have to check wiring and plumbing to make sure it's safe. Even if there are no termites, how sound is the structure? Building codes weren't as stringent that long ago."

"I know. I also know the real-estate business. I've had it checked out by an engineer. The house is sound, it just needs lots of work. But the beauty of it is how wonderful it will be when all renovated. Really our place—from our own hands."

"Not ours," he said, dashing her enthusiasm. "This is *your* project, from start to finish."

"You're not even going to look at it?" she asked, dismayed. She'd thought that once he saw it, he'd offer to help.

"I'll go see it," he said.

"Tomorrow?"

He nodded.

"In that case I'll stay here tonight and we'll go together," she said.

It was a small step, but she'd do anything to get back as a couple. It was not going to be an easy sell to him—he would deliberately put up barriers. But, given time, surely he'd come around?

The next morning, it was after nine when Annalise awoke. She never slept that late—or not until recently. She was constantly tired these days, and even yesterday's nap hadn't made much of a difference. She dressed quickly. Walking through the flat a short time later, she found she was alone. The coffeemaker was keeping the coffee hot. She took a cup and walked back to the living room to check outside. It was a beautiful autumn day. The sky was deep blue. She could see the trees below blowing in the wind. Crisp and clear, she expected. A perfect day for Dominic to see the house for the first time.

She hoped it would mend some of the breach between them. Last night had been downright awkward. She sipped her coffee and gazed out at the view of Washington that she loved. She would miss this when they moved.

Nothing had been settled. She still felt the distance between them. He was so unreasonable. Why wouldn't he at least consider the positive aspects of being a parent?

She called Dominic on his cell.

"Where are you?" she asked.

"I came into work. I'll be finished in an hour."

"We can pick up lunch somewhere and eat it at the house. It's too cold to eat outside, but I have that table and chairs, and the heat's turned on."

"I can hardly wait," he said dryly.

She ignored the trace of sarcasm in his voice. Maybe she'd go over early and get it looking the best it could for his first sight.

"I'll meet you there," she said, giving him quick directions. "I'll pick up sandwiches."

"Fine."

Annalise looked at the house more critically than normal when she turned into the driveway, trying to see it as if for the first time. It looked pretty bad. The yard was overgrown and unkempt. Compared to the neighbors' yards it looked appalling. The peeling paint detracted from any beauty in the structure itself. And that was just the outside.

Nothing she could do about that today. She hurried inside.

She heard his car when he arrived forty-five minutes later. Rushing to the front door, she could hardly wait to show him around. He *had* to like it!

Dominic got out slowly and did a scan of the yard.

"It needs work, of course," she said from the porch, feeling defensive. "But I figure Bridget can help us here. You know what a green thumb she has."

"This place needs a major overhaul. And, once done, how much upkeep will it require?" he asked, walking up the crumbling cement path.

"We'll put in low-maintenance plants. Hire a gardener to cut the grass. Sprinkler systems on timers. No work at all," she said quickly. She would not let Dominic's negative opinion dampen her enthusiasm.

She watched him study the house for a moment. The paint didn't look its best in the bright sunshine. Maybe she should have chosen an overcast day—or even rain. Dashing inside to keep dry might have been a better plan.

Annalise stepped aside for Dominic to enter. He halted inside, not saying a word.

She closed the door and walked into the living room. "This will be the lounge area. I picture it with comfy overstuffed furniture—all kid-proof, of course. I'd love curtains at the windows rather than blinds. And in blues and creams—sort of a country feel. Once the floors are redone, I'd get a big area rug, so it's warm underfoot in winter."

He looked at her. "We have modern furniture. Where does that go?"

"That goes with the flat. This would be decorated differently." She bit her lip as she stared at him. "We'd have to get new furniture."

He didn't say anything, but he looked at the floor that needed refinishing, the walls that needed painting, the windows that needed calking.

"Through here is the dining room—complete with table," she said as she led the way to the next room. The small table she had brought looked silly in the large room. "It needs a larger set, of course," she said, continuing through to the kitchen.

"This will be a showplace when we're finished," she said. "See the window over the sink? It looks out over the backyard. I can do the dishes and watch the kids. And once we get the yard fixed up we can have barbecues for family and friends."

She looked at him, waiting for his comments.

He looked around, walked to peer out the window. Turning slowly, he looked at her.

"This place is a dump, Annalise. It'll take tens of

thousands of dollars to get it habitable, much less decorated. The kitchen looks like it's from the 1940s. You have modern, state-of-the-art kitchen appliances in our flat. Why would you want this place?"

"It can be fixed up. It just needs new cabinets, new countertops, new appliances."

"Flooring, wall-covering, window-coverings and a new back door," he finished, looking at the old one. "So you spend a fortune to get what you already have now?"

"But the kitchen I have now is not in this house." She was trying to be reasonable, but Dominic was making her frustrated. Why couldn't he at least be the slightest bit open to the idea of a house? She wanted one for their baby.

"If the rest of the place is in as bad shape as the rooms I've seen, you've taken on an impossible task," he said.

"Look beyond what it is—see what it will be," she pleaded.

"It reminds me of the house I grew up in. You never saw it, since my dad moved to that apartment when I moved out. No one took care of the yard. My dad was too busy complaining about being stuck in that one-horse town to care about how the yard looked. The wallpaper was faded, having been put up two or three tenants before we moved in. My mother tried to keep the house clean, but it was old, damp, and it always needed repairs—most of which we were too poor to afford. Or my old man didn't care enough. This is an old house. Best torn down and a new house built on the lot."

"Our flat isn't all that new. The building is thirty years old."

"And it was completely renovated before we moved in. We didn't have to do anything but bring in furniture."

"You're not your father, and we don't live in some

one-horse town. And we have plenty of money to make the renovations." She could counter every argument he made. Why couldn't he at least give it a chance?

"I'm not interested in this house," he said.

She stared at him. "It can be a dream place."

"Maybe, with enough work. But it's not *my* dream place."

CHAPTER FOUR

ANNALISE blinked at that. She'd never truly considered that Dominic would not eventually come around to her way of thinking. Now she wasn't sure. That was happening a lot lately. Where was the man she'd thought she'd married, the man she could read and understand?

"What is your dream place?" she asked, fearing she already knew the answer.

"The flat we bought. Decorated the way we have it," he said.

"And that's all—for the rest of your life? That's *all* you want?"

She should not be so incredulous. If anyone had asked her a month ago she'd have said their flat was the perfect home. But that had been before she knew she was going to have a baby. Everything had changed. Just as Dominic had predicted.

"I'm hoping there's a long rest of my life, so I can't say that's all I'll want. But it's what I want now. I don't want reminders of the depressing place I grew up. I don't want to feel tied to a house when I could be flying to London. I don't want to paint and repair if we could be skiing in Aspen. The thought of mowing a lawn every weekend for the next fifty years is more than depressing."

Annalise looked out the window at the mess of a yard. She saw through the tangled bushes to a manicured lawn, toddlers running on the grass, she and Dominic sitting side by side as they watched with pride. Of course, that dream took some effort, with his reaction to her pregnancy.

"I'm sorry you see this like the home you grew up in. I see it as it can be—light and airy, and full of the aroma of chocolate-chip cookies baking. Kids running home from school to share their day. Laughter and love, family gatherings—just like my grandparents' homes."

"Are you sure you aren't romanticizing this? I know your parents' home was old-fashioned and made for children. Good thing, with all they had. But it's not for me."

He walked past her to enter the dining room, and stopped at the small table to start to unpack the lunch she'd bought.

When she followed, Annalise decided not to continue to talk about the house. Maybe Dominic would never come around. Maybe she was working on the house to fix it up for another family. Or, once it took shape, would he see it differently? She could consider different furnishings. Have one room like their flat—modern and minimal. She liked the sleek lines of their furnishings. The serene feeling of rooms without a lot of clutter. She could have a family room that housed the deep-cushioned furnishing, one that didn't need to be picked up every day but had children's toys strewn everywhere. Keep the two rooms separate.

"I don't want to fight. I don't want to be apart," she

said as she sat at the table. "I just want us to be like we've always been. If you don't like the house, let's consider it my personal project."

He sat and handed her a paper plate and a sandwich. "One that will take up an enormous amount of time and money. When do you propose we do things together?"

She admitted he had a point. She'd been spending all her available time while he was gone working on the house. And she had not accomplished as much as she thought she would. Everything took longer than she'd estimated.

"When you are home," she answered. She would have to schedule her renovations for the times he was gone. It would take longer to complete the project, but if he truly wasn't going to come around before the baby was born, her rush for completion vanished. Did she still even wish to proceed?

He didn't respond. After finishing half the sandwich, he wrapped the remainder in the paper and stuffed it back in the bag. "I'm done." Rising, he went to the stairs and climbed to the second story.

Annalise could follow his progress through the rooms from his footfalls. She'd have to think about carpeting on the second floor to help with the noise. They never heard their neighbors at the apartment building.

Her cell rang. It was her brother Sean.

"Hi, what's up?" she answered.

"I've been thinking about your request for help fixing up that monstrosity you bought."

"Changed your mind?" Things would go so much faster if she had help.

"Not me. Bunny's brother."

"A bunny's brother? Is this a crank call?"

"Bunny is the woman I'm seeing. It's her brother."

"The woman veterinarian you are seeing is named *Bunny?*"

"Yeah, I think it's kind of cute."

Annalise didn't want to tell her brother what *she* thought. "Her brother can help how?"

"He works in construction. There's not a lot of building going on now, so he has some free time—a couple of days a week anyway. I met him and thought he was okay. If you want, I can give you his number. I told him you might be calling."

"What's his name?" she asked suspiciously.

"Randall Hawthorne."

At least it was a normal-sounding name, she thought.

"Okay, give me his number. How much money does he charge? I don't have a lot after buying this place." She wasn't going to tell Sean that Dominic was against the project and would not be contributing. She wondered if she could manage it on her own. Did she still want to without his moral support?

Sean quoted her a figure and then rattled off the phone number. "It won't tally up to much if he only works one or two days a week," he added.

It sounded like a huge amount to her. But the sale she'd made last evening was bringing in a large commission. Maybe she could jump start the renovations with Randall's help. Dominic wouldn't see his old home in this place when it was renovated.

"I'll give him a call. Thanks. I still wish you'd help me out. You'd come a lot cheaper."

Sean laughed. "When you have the entire crew there, I'll come. But I'm not slave labor for you, baby sis."

Annalise and Lianne were the next in the line of children after firstborns Sean and Declan. Hardly the babies of the family.

She heard Dominic descending. "Got to go," she said to her brother, and rang off.

Dominic came to the doorway. "I've seen it all, and it's a mess. That bathroom's horrid. What were you thinking? Forget that—you weren't thinking. You couldn't possibly have considered all the expense and effort needed."

"That was Sean. He's found a contractor to help me out."

Dominic stared at her, wanting to understand what had happened to his wife. They'd been married for years—he would have sworn he understood her, that they were on the same wavelength. But this was mind-blowing. How she could rush out to buy this dump and then think it would end up as elegant as her grandparents' homes was beyond him. There was more work than an entire crew of O'Mallorys could handle in a year. And the upkeep once renovated would be tremendous.

Didn't she like the way they'd structured their lives? He enjoyed it, and he'd thought she did, as well.

He tried not to resent the baby. He'd been down that road once before. But if not for this pregnancy, things would have continued as they had over the last five years. Fate had a funny way of throwing a monkey wrench into the works. He knew he was in a different place this time. But the past reared its ugly memories and he had a hard time separating the two.

It also annoyed him that she had already lined up help with the project. Maybe she'd come to her senses sooner if she had to do it all on her own. His hope was that the longer she worked on it, the more money she poured into it, the sooner she'd realize what a drain it was and stop romanticizing home ownership. They already enjoyed all the benefits of owning a place, without all the maintenance and yardwork a family home would require.

Some people could see that for themselves. As *he* had, year after year with his parents. He knew some of his resistance to this house was an echo of his old man's complaints. Maybe he had cause. Dominic had never seen himself as a landscape gardener/general handyman—which a man needed to be to maintain a home in top shape. He knew from his construction work during college that he was competent enough as a carpenter, but he didn't enjoy it nearly as much as he liked using his mind to solve computer glitches.

The house wasn't the only problem. What were they going to do about the baby? The thought sent a shaft of panic blasting through him. That situation wasn't as easy to ignore as a house. He could feel the claustrophobia closing in. He needed to get away to be able to breathe.

"I don't know you anymore, Annalise. We've been together over six years, married five. And lately you are a total stranger to me."

She stared at him, her eyes large as she listened to the words. Was she really hearing what he was saying?

"I'm the same," she protested.

"No, nothing's the same. So where do we go from here?"

"You keep asking that."

"Because I never get a satisfactory answer," he said. He turned and walked out through the front door. Leaning against the railing of the porch, he took in a deep breath of the cool autumn air. She followed him.

"I think we should just take things as they come for now," she said, standing near him.

Dominic longed to pull her into his arms, to bury his face in the softness of her hair and hold her until his world settled itself. But *she* was the reason his world was cockeyed. Every time he thought about a baby it made him almost ill. He hated what that said about him, but he couldn't stop the feelings of claustrophobia that rose whenever he envisioned being tied down again. Having his future ransomed to an infant when he'd worked so hard to get where he was. He didn't want to grow to resent Annalise or a helpless baby. But if he couldn't find it in himself to become more excited about the new arrival, things would only get worse.

He had not changed. Maybe that was the key. Her pregnancy had altered the playing field. He had to decide to accept the situation, or cut and run.

"Maybe we should have a trial separation," he said at last.

The words tore at his heart. Yet it made sense. They had grown apart, were going in different directions. They might stay together for companionship, or from habit, but the spark of passion that bound them tightly, that made them a couple, had faded. Was that what had happened with them? Did he love her? She'd asked that question last night. He had been unable to shout out a definite yes. That scared him, as well. What *were* his feelings for her?

He looked at his wife. She had the same blue eyes and brown hair she'd always had. Her figure was trim and shapely. But the bright smile he liked so much was missing as she stared at him from sad eyes. What did he want from her? Instant denial of any separation? Some argument to convince him they belonged together? She wasn't giving him that. Maybe he wanted some acknowledgment that what he was asking for wasn't so off base. He'd made it clear from the beginning that he didn't see children in the picture.

"I don't want to. It'll change everything."

"The pregnancy has already changed everything," he said.

Tears spilled from her eyes, but he could tell she was trying to hold them back. One thing he could always say about Annalise: she never tried tricks to get her own way. He felt like the worst kind of heel. Yet he couldn't reconcile himself to the idea of becoming a father.

"Think about it. I'll see you if you decide to come home," he said, and turned to hurry to his car. He backed out of the driveway, noting the large trees that lined the street. "Leaves everywhere," he muttered, as he looked at the piles lining the sidewalks where diligent neighbors had raked them. "More work. Doesn't she see that? Owning a house ties a person down. I need to be free."

He drove home on autopilot. He could only think how Annalise had changed and he hadn't. Was that the problem? Was there something wrong with him that he couldn't see the wonder of having a baby? That he couldn't enthusiastically embrace owning a home? Was there something lacking in him? The something that made her so eager to expand their family and change their living arrangements, alter their entire lives?

Though in honesty he had to admit that initially she'd seemed as shocked as he to learn she was pregnant. She had reconciled herself to the fact faster. Now she seemed to welcome a baby into their lives, was willing to make monumental changes with enthusiasm. He wished he knew her secret.

Phyllis had not wanted to stay married to him once their reason for joining up in the first place had gone. Maybe there was a lack in him that women saw and he didn't. Things were spinning out of control. He had to hold on to his own dreams. If he was no longer enough for his wife as he was, what could he offer her?

Dominic let himself into the flat a short time later. He walked slowly into the living room. Stopping in the archway, he looked at the furniture they'd selected together. He remembered each shopping trip. They'd started with the console table and built from there. The sofa had been next. Then the coffee table. It had taken them months to find one they both agreed upon. He remembered the celebratory dinner they'd shared when they brought it home.

Piece by piece, he studied it, remembering. Even the flat itself held memories of their excitement the day they'd signed the papers. They'd come back after getting the key and made love in the bedroom, right on the floor.

Now she not only wanted to move, she wanted to change every stick of furniture. Virtually erase the past and start fresh with an entirely different style. Maybe it *was* time to end their marriage. For each to go their chosen way. The thought almost brought him to his knees.

Annalise watched in disbelief as the car drove off. She felt hollow inside. How dared Dominic just walk off and not fight for their marriage? Dozens of arguments sprang into her mind. She was not going peaceably away. If he thought they were over, he had another think coming.

Returning to the dining room, she cleaned up their

meal by rote, tossing the trash out and putting the remnants of their sandwiches in the fridge. Dominic drove her crazy. It wasn't *she* who wanted to separate. She was trying to adapt to the new circumstances. Was that so wrong? In a normal progression couples married, lived together for a while, then had children. Then the children would grow up and move out, and they'd be back to being a couple again.

It wasn't the horror story Dominic seemed to think it was. But without knowing more details about his first marriage she was hard-pressed to know how to counter his arguments. What two teenagers had faced was vastly different from a mature, successful married couple. Only, she suspected he was viewing the circumstances from those teenage eyes. And reacting to *those* circumstances—not the actual ones they faced.

If she'd thought she was angry before, she'd been fooling herself. She was so mad now she could spit nails. How *dare* he?

She flipped open her phone and called Lianne.

"Where are you?" she asked when her twin answered.

"Somewhere on I-95 between Richmond and Washington. Do you want me to ask Tray exactly where? He's driving."

"No. You'll be home in a couple of hours, right?"

"Probably about that."

"Come see me, will you? I'm at the house."

"What's up?"

"Dominic suggested a trial separation."

Annalise heard the hiss of surprise. "You're kidding," Lianne said.

"No. He hated the house—thinks I've gone off the deep end. And instead of trying to work with me, he just walked away." She took a breath. "I'm so angry I don't know what to do. Any suggestions? I'm afraid to call him up right now to let off steam. I might say something I'd later regret—but at the moment, I can't think of anything that I could say that I *would* regret. Damn him! It's not like I planned this baby—or had one with another man!"

"Whoa—I'll be there as soon as I can. Do you have your car?" Lianne asked.

"Yes."

"I'll have Tray drop me, and you can bring me home later," Lianne suggested.

"Okay, thanks. Tell him I owe him one."

"Give me the directions again. He says we'll be there in less than two hours."

Annalise paced around the room as she told her sister how to get to the house. Then she tossed the phone on the kitchen counter and went to work. She had to do something to expend her energy or explode.

She was too churned up over Dominic's comments to do more than hear his words echo again and again. Nothing had gone right between them for weeks. Was she a fool to think he'd come around? How could he not want a son or daughter? Their life was nothing like he described life in his hometown. She had thought *she* didn't want children, but now she was growing more and more excited about the prospect of having a baby. Of being a mother. What was wrong with Dominic?

"Annalise?" Lianne called.

"In the kitchen," Annalise called back, wiping her hands and heading for the front of the house.

Lianne waved to her husband, and Annalise heard the car drive away before her twin shut the front door.

"You should lock the door if you're here alone," Lianne said, slipping out of her jacket.

"It's a safe neighborhood. Thanks for coming."

Lianne glanced around and wrinkled her nose. "Cleaning didn't improve it much."

"Don't you start. Dominic thinks it a dump."

"He's got a point."

Annalise glared at Lianne, who simply shrugged and passed her sister on her way to the kitchen to put the tea kettle on.

"I assume you have an assortment of tea?" her sister said.

"Yes." Both twins loved tea—different kinds for different moods.

Once the water had boiled, Lianne prepared tea and poured them each a large mug full of chamomile.

"Any place to sit around here?"

"In the dining room, or on the bed upstairs."

"Dining room it is." Lianne led the way, and once they were both seated, she studied her sister for a moment. "For someone whose husband just left her, you seem remarkably cool about it."

"You should have been here two hours ago. I think smoke was coming out of my ears. He didn't leave, exactly. Just suggested a trial separation. Then said if I decided to come home, he'd be there. Like it's my decision."

"And are you okay with that?"

"Of course not! Nothing is going right. Becoming pregnant was just as much a surprise to me as to him. But I'm getting used to the idea. I can't imagine not having this baby now. But he doesn't seem to make any effort to see anything positive. And instead of talking things through, or making an effort, it's as if he's washing his hands of me and the baby."

"And he didn't like the house, I take it?"

"Says it reminds him of his childhood home—which I've recently found out he hated. Now that the truth is coming out, I realize how much he glossed over his past and how I let him. Now I want every detail. Only, he's thinking of ending our marriage. The jerk."

"And what do you want, sis?"

"I want this baby and my husband."

"So the giving him time part doesn't seem to be working—at least not in the short haul. He's still adamant?" Lianne asked, sipping her tea.

"He's horrified I bought the house. But this is the perfect family home. I want it fixed up so it's warm and welcoming and full of love and laughter. A place we'll live in for decades, like Grandma Carrie's home. I want family parties here. You know our flat is hardly big enough for the entire family. We never can sit down to dinner together there. It's always buffet-style."

"Face it, the only place anywhere near big enough for all of us at once is at the sea cottage. Once the rest of the family marries and maybe has a few kids there's not going to be a house large enough to seat us all at one time. I picture big barbecues at the beach on the sand."

"Or in our backyard. It's huge."

"Umm…" Lianne said.

"I have these pictures in my mind. Of me and Dominic sitting on the grass as a little kid learns to walk. Doesn't that sound as if everything is going to come out right? The backyard will be a perfect place for children to run around once it's tamed."

"And what does Dominic want?" Lianne asked.

"He wants nothing to change. I feel as if he's seeing his first wife when he looks at me. That he feels trapped by the mere thought of my pregnancy. But nothing is like it was when he was eighteen. Why can't he see that?"

Lianne shrugged.

"I probably would never have learned of his first marriage if I hadn't become pregnant. But history is not repeating itself like he thinks it is. Between that and his father, no wonder he doesn't want kids. But he sees other families—how can he think his experiences are the only way to be a family?"

"Because he can't truly relate?" Lianne offered.

Annalise tilted her head slightly while she brought up the memories she had of her father-in-law. They rarely visited him. "I never saw the house Dominic lived in when his mother was alive. I know Dominic doesn't like spending time with his father. Steve is a grumpy old man who is never satisfied with anything. I never really thought about growing up with someone like that before. I guess it could warp a person."

"But once that person is an adult, he no longer needs to play those childhood tapes over and over. People move beyond hardship in youth," Lianne said.

"So what do I do now? There is a baby on the way. I can't change that even if I wanted to, and I don't. I love this baby already."

"And you want this house," Lianne added, glancing around. "Though how you can see the potential is beyond me."

"Come back in a few months. You'll sing a different tune. Sean even has someone lined up to help me. If I can manage it financially." Annalise explained, and

Lianne burst out laughing when she told her about Sean's new woman-friend.

"It can't be serious," she said, her eyes dancing in amusement.

"Probably not—when is Sean ever serious? But if the guy can help me, that's all I care about."

"Forget the house. Concentrate on your husband."

"But what about me and what *I* want? It can't be all about what Dominic wants. What kind of marriage is that?" Though she missed him already. Or was it his support she longed for? Something to validate the choices she was making now? Where was the feeling she'd had of being one of a strongly bonded couple? She felt adrift. How often did trial separations end in reconciliation?

"Then you need to think about what kind of marriage you have. And where you want it to go."

"Not much of one if the first hiccup in the road of life has him suggesting a separation." She thought a moment. "We've had a wonderful five years—full and fulfilling. Lots of friends. We travel more than anyone I know."

"But how close are you two? I know you have a great life together, but where's the intimacy if he keeps major things in his past a secret?"

Annalise nodded, feeling hurt again at Dominic's revelation.

"You know, Lianne, the more I think about it, the more I think we had a fair-weather marriage. We both love entertaining. I like nice clothes, and I think he likes me looking nice when we go out. He's gorgeous, and I love being seen with him. But you're the one I go to with problems. What does that tell you about our relationship?"

"I know how he looks at you—as if he can't wait to get the two of you alone."

"There's never been a problem there," Annalise said pensively. "But is that enough for a strong marriage?"

"Who knows? But you have a history together, a basis to build upon. You have similar interests, similar passions. Find a way to reconnect. He's an only child from an unhappy marriage. Then he himself had an unhappy experience with marriage. Granted, he's been thrown in the midst of our family since day one, but at the end of the commotion and chaos you and he return to that ultra-serene flat and the tranquility that's there. No kids crying, no toys strewn everywhere. That's what he likes. And this expected baby threatens to change everything—from a couple to a threesome, and from a luxury apartment to a house that looks horrible right now. I'd be nervous about the entire situation myself," Lianne said.

"So what do you suggest?" Annalise asked.

"Make a fuss over him. I'm trying to keep Tray happy and not feeling second place to the baby, though you know how much I want this child. But I want Tray as my husband as much—if not more. I never thought I'd fall so deeply in love, but I have and it's wonderful."

"Sounds as if I'd be acting with an ulterior motive—butter him up to get my way," Annalise said. She looked at her sister. "I asked him if he loved me. He never answered."

"Men aren't as open with their feelings. You know that."

"A simple *Yes, I love you* would work," Annalise said. "What if he doesn't love me?"

"Then it's time you found that out," her sister said candidly. "You need to come to an agreement as a couple on how you'll face the future. Especially if he's to come around about the baby." Lianne looked around the room and made a face. "But I'm not sure he'll come around about the house."

Annalise took offense. "It's going to be a showplace when it's renovated."

"You keep seeing this place when it's all renovated. The rest of us see it as it is today, and it's a dump. And if he lived in poverty as a kid, this probably brings flashbacks which he doesn't want or need. When I suggested you go ahead with a home, I had no idea it would take so much work."

"Okay, I'll grant that maybe everyone doesn't have my vision. But, trust me, this is going to be wonderful. The perfect family home."

"If you say so," Lianne replied dubiously

The two sisters spent the remainder of the afternoon cleaning the upstairs bedrooms and discussing ways for Annalise to recapture Dominic's devotion. The talk segued into about how they felt being pregnant and what to name their babies. Not surprisingly, they both wanted the same name if their babies were girls—Caroline, in honor of their grandmother Carrie.

"So first girl born gets it?" Annalise said.

"When are you due?" Lianne asked suspiciously.

"Early June."

Lianne looked at her. "This is so weird. I'm due the first week of June. I can't believe we got pregnant at the same time."

"Twins," Annalise said, and they both laughed.

By the time Lianne had to leave for home, the cleaning was complete. Now the renovations could begin.

After dropping Lianne at her apartment, Annalise

called the number for Randall Hawthorne. He answered after three rings, and knew instantly who she was when she identified herself.

"My brother Sean said you might be available to help me renovate an old house," she said.

"My hours at the construction site have been cut due to the weather, so I have several days a week free. When do you need me?"

"I'm arranging my time so I can work on the house Friday, Saturday and Sunday. I figured working a block of days at a time would be better than spreading things out over the week."

"Sounds like a plan. I can do that."

They discussed what she could pay, what she wanted done.

"How about I come over now and check out the place, give you my suggestions on what to start first?" he offered.

"That would be great. The sooner the better. I don't have lights in all the rooms, so you need to see them before dark."

In less than half an hour Randall Hawthorne knocked on the door.

Annalise opened it, surprised at the young man standing there. He was as tall as Dominic, with sandy blond hair and an engaging grin. He was muscular from his work, and wore faded blue jeans and a ski jacket over his shirt.

"Randy Hawthorne, at your service," he said with an easy smile.

"I'm Annalise Fulton. Come in."

"Great old place. Man, this could really be cool when it's fixed up," he said as he gazed around the foyer and then into the living room. Stepping inside, he wandered around, running his hands lightly over the mantel, gazing out the window over the front porch. "But it's going to take a lot of work."

"Not more than I can handle, I hope," she said.

He turned and grinned at her. "Hey, you and me together can do a lot. Let's see the rest of the place."

Annalise showed him around, telling him what she envisioned for each room, with colors and repairs or, in the case of the kitchen, complete renovation.

When they ended up back in the foyer after the tour, Randy said, "I'd say get started on the front rooms first. They will be some of the easiest to do and you won't get discouraged. Once we have a few redone, we can tackle the kitchen and the bathrooms. Those are going to be the hardest and the most expensive. Leave them until later, so you'll start enjoying part of your handiwork long before we get to them."

"Okay." Annalise was pleased with his suggestions. She knew how she wanted everything to look at the end, but wasn't sure of the steps to get there. "What do we do first?"

They discussed the renovation plan for a while, deciding to start with the living room and dining room—beginning with refinishing the floors, painting the walls, and then thinking about furnishings.

"So, next Friday, early?" she said.

"I can be here at six."

"Oh, maybe not that early," she said, remembering how hard it was for her to get up these days. "Seven will be early enough. And I'll have the floor sander by then, so we can start right away."

When Randy had left, Annalise debated not returning to the flat. She knew there wouldn't be a warm welcome. But she wasn't going to be the one to leave this marriage. She'd try some of the tactics she and Lianne had discussed regarding Dominic. If their marriage was shaky, she was going to do her best to strengthen it. With or without Dominic's help!

CHAPTER FIVE

IT WAS late by the time Annalise returned to the apartment. Dominic was in the den. She peeked in at him, but he was working on the computer and barely acknowledged her greeting. She went to take a shower and dressed in her sexiest nightie. It was a little cool in the apartment, but she hoped that would change. Slipping on a silky robe, she went to the kitchen and prepared some hot chocolate.

Carrying two mugs into the den, she set one down near Dominic on the desk.

"Hot chocolate. Take a break."

"Sounds good," he said, reaching for the mug. He glanced at her and his eyes held. Slowly he moved his gaze down her body, seeing the robe part slightly when she sat on the small chair near the desk, her slender legs revealed.

He looked away, taking a swallow of the hot beverage and then exclaiming when it burned his mouth.

"Careful—it's hot."

"So, it appears, are you," he said, looking back.

She could see desire in his eyes, the way they darkened and went so smoky. Her own pulse increased.

"I was when I got out of the shower, but it's cool in here."

He carefully sipped his chocolate. Annalise wanted to smile. She could almost see the calculations in his mind. Carefully, Dominic put down his mug and rose. He held out his hand for hers. She had not even had a sip, but gladly relinquished it.

"Come to bed," she said, rising.

"My pleasure," he said, leaning in to kiss her.

Pleasantly tired some time later, Annalise relished snuggling against her husband. She'd fall asleep in another moment, but she wanted to savor the afterglow. There was more to resolve, answers to get, but for the moment, she was with Dominic, and it was enough.

"Tell me about Phyllis," she said. Instantly she felt him tense.

"What's to tell?"

"Everything. You said you were high-school sweethearts?"

"We dated. Hung out together when I wasn't working. Even then I was trying to save enough for college. I had a scholarship to Penn, but knew I'd need more money to make it."

"Did she plan on college?"

"No."

"What was she going to do?"

"I don't remember," he said slowly. He was silent for a moment.

"What was she like?" Annalise asked.

"Small, dark. She changed after high school—after we were married."

"How?"

"Different ways. Before we seemed to get on okay. But once we were married, when she was pregnant, she became clingy. Never wanted me out of her sight. She used her condition to manipulate everything to go her way. We couldn't go to the movies because we had to save for the baby. Couldn't have friends in—our apartment was too small and crummy, and what could we serve them? She'd spend hours reading books about babies."

"Sounds as if she was scared."

"I never thought so then."

"What would you know? You weren't going to be a mother at eighteen," Annalise said softly.

"I knew I was scared we wouldn't make it. The dead-end job at the mill was boring and tedious, but it brought me a paycheck. God, I hated that job. Phyllis managed the money and did it well. We had no debts, managed to have food on the table every meal. But the thought of doing that for another fifty years about drove me insane."

"You were both too young to have a baby," Annalise said.

"Well, we didn't, did we?" he said, sitting up.

"Dominic, you did not cause that baby to be still-born," she said, sitting up, as well.

"You don't know everything, Annalise. Maybe thoughts *can* influence an outcome. The intensity of my desire to be free was almost tangible. How do you know it didn't penetrate Phyllis some way and end that baby's life."

"Come on—don't be like that. You did not do anything wrong."

"I did it all wrong." He stood and went to pull on a pair of jeans. Grabbing a shirt from the closet, he stormed out of the bedroom.

Annalise debated following him, but decided against it. She'd pushed a lot, and he'd responded. Now she'd brought it all to the forefront. What would he do next?

* * *

Dominic went to the kitchen and poured himself a drink. He usually only drank socially at parties, but tonight he wanted the burn of alcohol, the forgetfulness it could bring. He'd worked so hard to forget that year. Annalise couldn't understand how awful things had been. Phyllis had changed from the girl he'd gone out with throughout the last two years of high school to a whiny, clinging girl who wouldn't give him any space.

In retrospect, he hadn't handled it well. He'd been resentful of losing his chance at college, angry at finding only the job at the mill and scared as he'd told Annalise. He'd known nothing then about being a father, and he knew nothing now.

He stood in the dark and let the memories wash through him. Each one strengthened his resolve. He could not go through that again. He didn't want his feelings for his wife to turn into bitter resentment. He didn't want to see Annalise become clingy. He had come as far from that life as he could get. To be sucked down into a repeat was not in the cards.

Yet Annalise was right. Stay or go, he'd still be a father. What kind of man wasn't there for his child? Even his old man had always been there—complaining every moment, but there. Once again he'd do his duty. And count the years until he could be free.

The next morning, Annalise woke late and rushed getting dressed and dashing to the office. Dominic was already gone. She had appointments lined up all day and didn't have a moment to worry about her personal life.

Midafternoon, she took a break and called Dominic's cell.

"Fulton," he answered. As always, her heart skipped

a beat at just hearing his voice. How could he even suggest a trial separation? She wanted to be closer, not drift apart. Yet now that the specter had been raised she began to question every aspect of their marriage. Last night had been glorious, until she'd brought up his first wife. He had not returned to their bed after he'd left.

And she could not forget that he had not answered her question the other night.

"Hi," she said, wishing the breach between them could be miraculously healed.

"Hi, yourself." He sounded like the old Dominic.

"Want to meet for Chinese dinner?' she asked.

"What time?"

"My last showing is at four. So, unless they decide to buy on the spot, I could make it around six-thirty."

"See you then," he said.

As she hung up, she considered that maybe Lianne was right. She needed to show Dominic that nothing had changed as far as the two of them were concerned just because a baby was expected. She would always make time for her husband. They'd still eat out, go to a show, entertain. Maybe she should plan another party.

But when? She was guarding her weekends jealously. That was the only time she had to work on the house.

Thinking about that had her wanting to call Mary Margaret. Did her sister put her children first, to the detriment of her husband? But she couldn't call and ask— first of all it would insult her sister, and second no one knew about her pregnancy but Lianne. Maybe Annalise should call her parents and announce the news and have done with it.

But not until Dominic was reconciled to the idea.

Annalise arrived at their favorite Chinese restaurant

promptly at six-thirty. She entered, and saw Dominic lounging against the wall in the narrow entryway.

"Did I keep you waiting?" she asked, reaching up to kiss him.

"Just got here a minute ago." He turned and nodded to the hostess.

Annalise was a bit disappointed he hadn't returned her kiss with more fervor, but they were in a public place—though Dominic had never been that reticent when they'd first married. And usually he held her hand or flung an arm over her shoulder. Tonight they could pass for business colleagues going to dinner.

The waitress seated them in a booth near the front. It was quiet and dimly lit. Handing them menus, she went to get the hot tea.

"Let's get the same thing as always," she said, leaving the menu closed near the table's edge.

"Suits me," he said.

The same as always comprised Szechuan beef, kung pao chicken and pork chow mein. They had discovered early in their relationship that they had similar tastes in food.

"So how was your day?" Annalise asked brightly. She could have kicked herself. That sounded so first date-ish. Were they down to banalities? She wanted to establish their old rapport before demanding answers to questions about Phyllis and the life they'd led. Or finding out more about the child who had not lived.

Dominic's eyes flashed amusement. "Fine. How was your day?"

"Okay, that was dumb. What's going on at work?"

"We have a new client in Maryland. I may have to go up there later in the week, to get an overview of the computer setup. They are a startup security firm in Annapolis and are bidding for a contract with the Navy, so are beefing up their own security to show the Navy they are up to the task they're bidding for."

"I'd think you could tell that from dialing into their system."

"Most of it I can, but I want to check out the physical layout and see what security procedures they have to protect the mainframe. Backup measures, that kind of thing."

"What else?"

He smiled slightly. "I played games."

She nodded. When Dominic said he played games, he didn't mean the kind she played on computers. His firm had some of the brightest minds in the world as employees. They constantly tried to trip up one another through altered codes on existing programs. It kept them on their toes, devising problems and then solving them.

"What about you?" Dominic asked.

"I showed the Worthys two more houses. I swear, they have seen every house in the north-east section, the north-west and near the Capitol. Neither of these was quite right, either. I think they like looking at houses, but I'm beginning to think they are not seriously looking, and have no intention of buying."

"Do what you did with that other couple who only wanted to look. Get the credit report and the mortgage pre-approved before showing them any more."

"I think I will. That usually separates the men from the boys," she said.

The waitress showed up with their meal, and for the next few moments, they were quiet as they ate. Annalise was beginning to feel as if they'd regained their old footing. She looked up and feasted her gaze on Dominic for a moment. She still thought he was the best-looking man she'd ever seen. His dark eyes flicked up and met hers, holding her gaze for a moment. She could feel the quiver of anticipation shoot through her. Would they return to the flat and make love?

"So what does Lianne think of your house project?" he asked, as if deliberately thrusting a wedge between them.

Annalise's heart sank. Anytime the house or baby came up it widened the distance between them.

"She shares your opinion that it's a dump."

"Enlightened woman," he murmured.

"You both have no imagination. It's going to be beautiful. You'll see. And I'm starting on Friday. I've hired a construction worker to help me."

"Who?" Dominic went on the alert.

"The brother of the girl Sean is seeing. He came by the house on Sunday and I hired him. *He* thinks the house is going to be beautiful when it's done." And so far Randy was the only one besides her that did.

"What do you think you're doing? You shouldn't have had him out to the house with only you there," Dominic said, leaning closer and glaring at her. "He could have been a mass murderer or something."

"I told you, he's Bunny's brother."

Dominic looked at her for a moment. "Bunny?"

"Sean's latest. The vet. Her name is Bunny."

"And what's her brother's name? Doggie?"

Annalise wanted to giggle, but she was miffed Dominic had acted as if she didn't know what she was doing. She'd bought this house on her own. She was directing the renovations. She knew exactly what she was doing. And if the man had been anyone other than the brother of Sean's girlfriend, she *wouldn't* have had him at the house when she was there alone. Though she was constantly showing homes to strangers. Which Dominic also had a problem with. Maybe he was just being protective.

"His name is Randy and he works in construction, but not so much now that the weather is bad. He had some great ideas and we start on Friday." She kept her tone reasonable.

Dominic was quiet for a moment. "I thought I'd go to Annapolis on Friday and you could go with me. After I visit the new client we could find a bed and breakfast and stay the weekend. Wander around the old part of town."

She was torn. A trip to Annapolis sounded wonderful. And she'd have a chance to build a bridge over the chasm that seemed to grow wider each time they were together. But she'd already committed to Randy to start on the house. Time truly was not on her side. If the weather got too inclement they would have to delay some of the repairs to the windows, and wouldn't be able to paint and air out the place.

"I wish I had known earlier. I'm sorry, but I can't make it. I've reserved a floor sander, and Randy will be there early on Friday to start. The weekends are the only time I'll have to get this house in shape before the baby comes. I won't be able to go anywhere for a while."

She hated seeing the flash of anger in his eyes.

"Maybe I could take another day during the week," she offered. It would mean the possible loss of revenue, but there was no sure sale in the works, so she'd be glad to chance that.

"I'm busy until Friday," he said, sitting back and finishing the last of his tea. "Ready to leave?"

She nodded. So much for building bridges. Why

hadn't she been more amenable to his suggestion? Was it pride? Or resentment that he wouldn't see things her way? She was mad he seemed to make no effort to change.

When they returned home, Dominic closed himself in the den. Disappointed that the evening that had started so promising had turned out badly, Annalise pulled out her laptop and connected to the Internet, reading how-to articles on refinishing floors and woodwork. She wanted the knowledge if not the experience when she and Randy began work on Friday.

The next morning, Annalise overslept again. She hoped she would not be this tired all through her pregnancy. She scrambled to make it to her first appointment, and the day was hectic, with home tours from the office and two new listings to be signed. She had a strong clientele in the area, and word of mouth expanded it each year. She loved showing homes and making suggestions on creative financing. She had a solid base of happy homeowners who had bought through her. Some had become friends and they often saw each other.

Thinking about it, she should be planning another party for December. Would Dominic be available? She called him.

"I am already too late for a party in early November. And then we run into Thanksgiving. But what about a party that first weekend in December? Will you be here?" she asked as soon as he answered.

"Do you have time? What about your house?"

"Stop antagonizing me. I can't go with you this weekend because I made prior plans. But with enough notice I can do almost anything. We always have a party or two this time of year. But before I reserve caterers and all I want to make sure you'll be home."

"I'll mark down that first Saturday. Can't guarantee it, but I'll do my best."

"Perfect. We can review the guest list tonight and I'll start with invitations—December gets full really fast. We'll get a jump on the others."

Getting home a bit early, she prepared a nice dinner. They'd eat, plan the party, and fall back into their normal routine.

By seven, however, Annalise gave up on Dominic showing up. She'd called his cell, but it was inactive. Had he deliberately turned it off, or had the battery run down? That rarely happened, but it did once in a while if he was too involved with other things.

Was he playing his games again? She was constantly amazed at how he and his other computer coworkers could get lost for hours in tracing codes to find a problem. It sharpened their diagnostic skills. Dominic was a natural at it—with an intuitive concept of problems. She was fascinated with the way he thought.

She ate, and put Dominic's portion on a plate in the fridge to be heated when he got home. Going to the den when she'd finished, she drafted a list of friends and relatives she'd invite to the party. Knowing she'd have to cut down on entertainment for a while afterwards, she listed more people than she could handle with a buffet. So this one would be only a cocktail party, with hors d'oeuvres. Leaving the names on the desk for Dominic to review, she went to bed.

The next night when Dominic didn't come home before she was ready to go to bed, Annalise was fed up. She packed up a few items, left him a note and headed for the house. If he didn't want to spend time with her, she'd show him what a trial separation was really like. It might bring him to his senses.

It could backfire and she'd find he loved being on his own. But that was a chance she'd have to take. After making love so ardently earlier in the week, she knew there was still that spark of attraction between them. Maybe Dominic needed to pay more attention to that than dwell on the past.

He did not call on Thursday.

Friday, Annalise woke excited at finally beginning work on the house. She made coffee and heated bagels, and was eating the small meal when she heard Randy pull into the driveway.

It was cold, and threatening rain, but to Annalise the day was rosy with promise. She would begin actual renovations today! She hurried out to meet her new helper.

Annalise had rented the floor sander, which had been delivered yesterday afternoon. It sat in the center of the living room.

"Know how to work that?" she asked Randy when they entered that room.

"Sure."

In no time he was sanding the scarred wooden floors, while she hand-sanded the woodwork around the windows. By lunchtime her hand ached from holding the sander, and her shoulder hurt from the repetitive motion. But the windows were ready to be primed. She only had the mantel around the fireplace to finish and this room would be ready for paint. Randy was almost finished with the large floor in the living room.

"I'll make a sandwich run," she said, rotating her shoulders to try and ease the ache.

"Works for me. I'll be finished here soon, and ready to do the dining room after lunch. And then the entry hall. Stairs will have to wait."

"I think I'll carpet them, so we don't need to redo," she said, studying the stairs. Carpet would make it quieter, so not to hear the clatter of children running up and down. She planned to carpet the upstairs rooms for the same reason.

After a congenial lunch, they resumed their tasks. Once she finished the mantel, she vacuumed up the grit and washed everything down to minimize the dust. She wanted the floors to be silky smooth. Randy had told her they needed to get all the dust up and wait for it to settle out of the air. Then do another sweep with tacky cloth. Tomorrow they'd be able to begin staining.

Randy left around six, and Annalise ate another sandwich for dinner. She went shopping for more groceries afterward, and then watched a silly show on television before going to bed. She wondered how Dominic was enjoying Annapolis. She was hurt he hadn't called to see how she was doing. Maybe leaving had been a mistake.

Saturday, she had breakfast ready when Randy arrived. They ate quickly and she put the dishes in the sink, running hot water over them. She'd clean up later. Now they needed to get started on the final wipe-down and staining the wood. She was excited to see the room transformed. Randy had been right. It would be gratifying to have one completed so soon.

Randy showed her how to brush the stain on the wooden floor in the direction of the grain and then wipe off the excess, repeating until she got the perfect shade. When the stain dried, they'd seal it, and the floor would be beautiful for many years to come.

It was easier than Annalise had anticipated. She chatted with Randy, learning more about his sister. Did he believe Sean was serious? They discussed jobs he'd worked on, finding a house she'd sold a couple of years ago had been one he'd renovated.

When they were halfway through the living room, Annalise heard a car in the driveway.

"Who can that be?" she murmured. *Darn,* she didn't want to stop.

CHAPTER SIX

FOOTFALLS sounded on the porch, then the front door opened.

"Annalise?" Dominic called.

"Oh," she said, looking at the floor. She was on the left side of the room, with Randy on the right. They were half-way through, and wanted to complete it by lunchtime.

"Friend of yours?" Randy asked, still working.

"Husband. In here, Dominic," she called.

When he reached the archway, she sat back on her heels and looked at him. "Don't come in. We're staining."

He looked at Randy, then at the floor that had been stained.

"I thought you went to Annapolis," Annalise said. What was he doing here?

"I came home last night." He looked at Randy again.

"Randy, this is my husband, Dominic Fulton. Dominic, Randy Hawthorne. He and I are staining the floor," Annalise said, hoping to defuse the tension that seemed to be growing.

"I can see that," Dominic said, not taking his eyes off the construction worker.

"Hey, man," Randy said with an easy grin. "I'd get up to shake hands, but don't want to interrupt the rhythm."

"Annalise, can I see you a moment?" Dominic asked.

"I'm kind of busy right now. Can it wait another hour or so? We'll be finished by then."

Ignore her for three days and then expect her to jump when he said so? Not by a long shot, she thought, annoyed he'd shown up when she was in the middle of a project.

Dominic looked at his wife and the man, working diligently on their staining. They had accomplished a lot already. The trim around the windows had been stained the same color as the floor. The carved wooden mantel looked as new as it had eighty years ago. The floors would turn out nice. No slacker here.

But he didn't like the idea of Annalise working closely with this man. If he'd been fifty and balding, maybe. But Randy Hawthorne looked young and fit and too friendly by half.

"I'll wait," he said.

"We're doing the dining room after lunch," she said, carefully applying the brush and then wiping away the excess stain. Already ignoring him.

With another glance at Randy, Dominic asked, "Got coffee?"

"Some instant in the kitchen. We drank the other already."

He walked through the dining room, noting how nicely the floors had been sanded. Not Annalise's work, he knew; she wasn't skillful enough to sand a floor so evenly. He reached the kitchen and put on a kettle. Looking in the cupboard for coffee, he noticed the dishes in the sink. Two sets. How cozy.

Dammit, she was his *wife*. What was she doing eating meals with another man?

When he'd suggested a separation, he'd expected her to fight tooth and nail to stay together. Seemed as if she was doing just fine on her own. Didn't she miss him?

He missed her like crazy. He'd come here today to talk some sense into her. She had made her point. Now she could come home.

And not a moment too soon if she was taking her meals with some stranger.

Probably part of the pay for this construction worker. Whom she wouldn't have needed to hire if she hadn't bought the damn house.

Or if he had helped. He'd worked in construction for six summers, from high school through college. He knew enough about building to manage this place. And what he didn't know he could learn—a lot easier than Annalise.

But he didn't want to work on this house. If it hadn't been for the house she would have gone with him to Annapolis. It was as if she had a split personality—the woman he'd married, and a stranger bent on having babies and renovating old homes. He *wouldn't* encourage her to fix the house up. That would have her even more determined to live in it. Their flat had all they needed.

Except a nursery, came the unbidden thought.

He clenched his jaw at the reminder and gazed out the back window while the water heated. He did not like the yard. Sure, they could hire a gardener, but he still didn't like the idea of being responsible for a lawn and a garden.

He disliked the idea of his wife turning to someone else even more.

He fixed the coffee and wandered back to the archway. Annalise was on her knees, and when she leaned over her sweetly rounded rear rose in the air. Randy worked beside her, so he couldn't see, but Dominic didn't like their camaraderie, either.

Get used to seeing her with another man if you leave, he told himself. And hated the very idea. Annalise was *his*.

Randy was telling Annalise about a fishing trip he'd been on, and she was laughing at his story. She knew enough about the subject to discuss lures and flies with him. Dominic leaned against the doorjamb and grew more frustrated as the minutes ticked by.

"You do much fishing?" Randy asked over his shoulder to Dominic.

"Sea-fishing in the summer, sometimes."

"One of my brothers has a boat, and we go out with him," Annalise explained.

The man nodded. He was almost finished with his portion of the floor, and undoubtedly would be helping with Annalise's side when he'd done.

They bumped into each other. Dominic could tell it wasn't intentional, but it still made him want to reach out and grab the man.

"I have some vacation time coming. I could help here," he said. Almost as soon as the words were out he wished he could recall them. He did not *want* to work on this house—he would be giving mixed messages if he did. Annalise would think he was softening in his stance against the place. But he sure wouldn't tell her it was because he was jealous of the smiles she gave that man.

Randy looked up and grinned. "Hey, man, that's cool. With three of us working we can get this place fixed up in no time. I was telling Annalise her ideas are terrific. This is going to be a showplace. I can't wait to see it, can you?"

"I can't wait," Dominic said. So Randy had bought into Annalise's scheme. Or was he just saying what his employer wanted to hear?

Annalise rocked back on her heels and looked at Dominic. "I thought you didn't want anything to do with this place."

"Well, I changed my mind." His look challenged her to argue. She was so pretty, even in old clothes and with brown stain on her fingers. He wanted to snatch her up and take her to the bed upstairs. Hardly likely with Randy around.

"Fine. We can use the help." She resumed the staining.

"I'll go home and change clothes and be back this afternoon," he said a moment later. "Shall I pick up lunch?"

"Get yourself something. I have enough for me and Randy," she said.

Dominic almost told her Randy could go out and find his own food, but he held back. Things were too tenuous between them to give vent to how he really felt.

Driving back to the flat, Dominic acknowledged he was jealous of the man working so well with his wife. He'd never minded her colleagues at the real-estate office or the men she knew in finance and banking. But none of those had ever represented a threat in Dominic's mind. Randy liked her idea of the house. That was heady stuff when her own husband was so against it.

Randy was also young and good-looking. Dominic suppressed the anger that rose at the thought of him coming on to Annalise. She wasn't going to be distracted by some guy, even if he *was* good-looking. Unless she felt neglected by her own husband. Which of course, she did. She'd made overtures last week and he'd rebuffed them. Now it was his turn. He hoped she would be more generous.

But he couldn't seem to get by his feeling of history repeating itself. And he did not want that. He didn't know what he wanted. That was the problem. Being in San Francisco without her had made him realize how much she was a part of his life. They enjoyed the same shows, books, movies. They liked to wander around historic parts of different cities. Their taste in food was similar. They had a good marriage. Two people who liked the same things.

Do you love me? The thought came unexpectedly.

He'd tried to evade the question, but it echoed in his mind. What was love?

Two people, two good friends, doing things together— only more? They had so much in common. He wouldn't give up their intimacy for anything. Yet wasn't he suggesting that very thing with a trial separation?

What was love? A yearning to be with a special person? He could ask her the same question. Only she hadn't been the one to suggest separation.

When Dominic returned an hour later, wearing old jeans and a shirt that had seen better days, he heard laughter from the kitchen and walked through the now empty dining room to find Randy and Annalise sitting at the small table.

She looked up at Dominic, the smile lingering in her eyes.

He felt the flare of desire he always had around her. And a curious hunger for more. To know her thoughts, her fears, her hopes and dreams. And where he fit in each of them.

"I'm finished, if you want to sit at the table," Annalise said. There were only two chairs.

"No, I ate as I drove. What's scheduled for this afternoon?" He'd find a way to get her alone for a serious discussion. If he helped with the renovations, she wouldn't need to hire another man.

"We're going to stain the dining-room-window trim and the floor." She held up her hands, dark brown from the color they were using. "I hope that's the end of it. I'll have to soak my hands in bleach for a month to get them clean again."

"Naw, I've some stuff in the truck that'll take that right off," Randy said.

"Good. I'd hate to have walnut-brown hands the rest of my life." She grinned at him.

Dominic drew in a sharp breath. He wanted his wife smiling at *him* like that again.

"Should you be working around these fumes?" he asked. He walked closer, put his hand on her shoulder. "She's pregnant, you know," he told Randy. It was primitive—like he was staking his claim. Which he was.

"No? Really? Bunny didn't say. Cool. Congrats to you both. Wow, a little rug rat. Your first?" Randy seemed genuinely pleased with the news.

Annalise nodded, smiling. She threw a wary glance at Dominic.

Another notch against the man. He was as excited about the news as Annalise's family was going to be. Obviously he didn't have any of his own, Dominic thought cynically. Nor did he know what havoc babies could cause in people's lives.

"I'm due next summer. I'm hoping to have the house finished by then," she said.

"Cool. We'll do it. Especially with your husband's help. Annalise has bragged on you, man. Said you worked years in construction. Between us we should knock it out in no time," Randy said.

"Cool," Annalise repeated.

Dominic wanted to grind his back teeth. He put his hands in his jeans pockets and faced Randy. "I thought I could do Annalise's shift on the staining, and she could do something easier, away from the fumes," he said. He'd rather be paired with Randy-the-friendly than have his wife working with him all afternoon.

"I'll get started upstairs," she said, jumping up and taking the remnants of her lunch to the trash. She put the dish in the sink. "First I'll do these dishes and start the crockpot for dinner." She looked at Dominic uncertainly. "Will you be here for dinner?"

"Of course," he said, before Randy could say a word. He was going to make sure the man knew his wife was off-limits.

Annalise looked at her husband in surprise. There was no *of course* about anything he did anymore. And nothing could have surprised her more than having him show up today and volunteer to work on the project. And announce her pregnancy to Randy. She looked between the two men and wondered if something was going on that she was unaware of.

She grabbed some more sandpaper and walked up the stairs, wondering how long this offer of extra help would last. She'd take all she could get. But it was odd he'd waited until Randy had started.

It couldn't be because he was jealous. Dominic knew he would never have reason to be jealous of anyone. She had loved him since she'd first met him. Even now, when he was being infuriating. She wished Randy would leave and Dominic would come up to the bedroom with the bed in it. Dreaming the afternoon away, she sanded until her arm was numb.

When she could do no more, she sat on the floor and dialed her sister Bridget's phone.

"How would you like the wonderful opportunity to design a garden from beginning to end—design to planting?" she said, when Bridget answered.

"What's the catch?" her sister asked.

"None. I've bought a house that has a disaster of a yard. I envision a lush lawn and colorful flowers, but haven't a clue even where to start. You have always loved gardens. How many hours have you spent in Grandma Carrie's garden? And your own? Here's your chance to design one however you like—the only caveat is to keep it easy to maintain."

"I heard you bought a house. When can I see it?"

"Anytime. I'm here this weekend, and as many weekends as I can manage."

"I'll come by tomorrow around noon—that work?"

"Perfect."

"So what's up with the parents?" Bridget asked.

"Nothing that I know of. Why?"

"Mom called earlier to see if I was free next weekend. I'm home, and she said she'd call back when they'd firmed things up. So I asked her what, but she just blew me off."

"She hasn't said anything to me. Maybe it's something special for you."

"It's not my birthday, so what else could it be?"

"Any promotion at work that deserves a celebration or something?"

"*Nada.* Well, if she calls you, let me know. See you tomorrow."

Annalise finished sanding the trim in the front bed-room and then went to the room in the back that held the bed. She'd lie down just for a minute. Her entire right side ached now. She needed to work into fixing this place up gradually. There was no need to attempt to do everything this weekend.

On that thought she promptly fell asleep.

"Annalise?" Dominic shook her gently.

She opened her eyes. It was dark outside. The faint illumination from the hall light showed her husband leaning over her.

"Are you all right?" he asked.

"Just tired. And my arm hurts from sanding so much these last two days. No wonder Randy is in such good condition. This is hard physical work!"

"Yeah, well, you shouldn't push yourself so much."

"Pace myself? Good idea. Only there's so much to do, and I'm anxious to have it all completed."

"Dinner's ready. Your construction friend left. He had a date," Dominic said.

"Oh? How late is it?"

"After seven."

She groaned and sat up, still feeling as if she could sleep a week.

"I can dish up the dinner and bring it up, if you'd rather stay here," he said, stepping back to give her space to rise.

"No, I'll be right there." She hated to move. Truth-fully, there was nothing she'd like more than to roll over and go back to sleep. But she needed to eat.

Walking down the stairs, she surveyed the floors of the main level.

"They look beautiful," she said, stepping gingerly on the foyer portion.

"They're dry. Tomorrow we'll seal them and let that dry for a week, then give a second coat next Sunday. But you can walk on them carefully in the meantime."

"Thank you for your help. I know the work will go faster with the two of you in charge. I lack your experience."

Dominic made a noncommittal sound and led the way into the kitchen. The aroma of the stew in the crockpot filled the air. She was instantly starving. Using the few plates and utensils she'd brought, they soon began eating.

"This tastes so good," she said, watching in satisfaction as her husband gave every appearance of enjoying his meal. The old adage came to mind. The way to a man's heart is through his stomach. Maybe this was a way to remind him of all they had? He wasn't much of a cook. Before they'd married he had made do with fast food and hamburgers—typical college fare. Her mother had taught her how to prepare meals of all kinds, and Dominic liked the food she made. Obviously including tonight.

"What's up for tomorrow?" she asked.

"We'll tackle that little room behind the living room, and then seal the floors. Once that's done, no walking on them for at least twenty-four hours."

"Bridget's coming over at noon to see the yard. I asked her to landscape. How long will it take you and Randy to seal the floors?"

"A couple of hours, max."

"Next weekend I can paint the living and dining room walls, right?"

He nodded.

She took another bite. If she couldn't walk on the floors while the top coat dried, where would she go?

Glancing at him, she considered returning home. Then promptly vetoed the idea. First of all, she wanted him to ask her back. She needed that. It wouldn't be much of a statement if she headed for home the first time something came up. She didn't need Dominic. She wanted him—as husband, lover, father to her baby. But if that was not to be, she could manage on her own. Time her husband realized that.

It didn't take long to do the dishes when they'd finished.

"Ready to go home?" he asked casually, hanging up the drying towel.

"I am home," she said, turning to face him. "You wanted a trial separation, you've got it."

"Okay, we tried it. I don't like it."

She shrugged, holding his gaze.

"What do you want?" he asked.

"Some assurance we are going to make it," she said.

"There are no guarantees in life."

"That's reassuring," she replied dryly.

"Look, I know we're stuck with the baby. I have to make the best of it."

"Get out, Dominic. Wrong answer, wrong attitude— wrong, wrong, wrong *everything*."

She pushed past him and headed upstairs, slamming the bedroom door when she'd entered the room. She held her breath, waiting for some indication he wasn't going to let the situation remain as it was.

The sound of his car gave her the answer. Not the one she wanted.

She flipped open her phone and called Lianne.

"Can I stay with you this week?" she asked, when her sister answered the phone.

"Oh-oh—trouble in river city?"

"Maybe, maybe not." Annalise explained about moving out, and then about Dominic showing up to help her today. "I think he's surprised I'm not like his first wife."

"And how is that?"

"Dependent."

Lianne laughed. "That does not sound like you. He's known you for years—does he really think you'll become dependent?"

"Apparently his first wife did when she became pregnant." Annalise could say the words *first wife* without a pang. She was accepting the past, growing used to it. Maybe she'd never know the full story about their relationship, but as long as it remained in the past she would not dwell on it. What had happened before she met him went into making him the man he was today—hang-ups and all.

"So what's the plan?"

"I'm living in the house until further notice. Only, they are sealing the floors on the main part of the house tomorrow, and I can't walk on them for a while. So I'd need to stay with you for several nights."

"You are always welcome here, sis, you know that," Lianne said. "And I want to hear more about Dominic's first wife."

"I'll tell you all I know—which still is hardly anything."

"See you when you get here," Lianne said.

Annalise went to bed more content than she'd been in days. Dominic had come to help on the house. That meant a lot.

By the time Bridget arrived the next day, Annalise was glad to escape to the yard. She'd tried to help with the flooring, but Dominic didn't want her around the fumes. Randy and Dominic seemed to have an armed truce between them. They were cordial enough, but neither seemed to like the other much. Were they disagreeing on how to do the job?

It was her house, and she wanted to make sure things got done the way she wanted, but at one point even Randy said they'd do more faster if she'd get out of their way.

She was sitting on the front porch, imagining what the garden could look like, when her sister turned into the driveway. There was scarcely room for her vehicle with their own two cars and Randy's truck. Bridget climbed out of her low-slung sports car and headed up the crumbling walkway.

"Wow, this is fantastic," she called, when she spotted Annalise. "And I get to do whatever I want?"

"As long as I can afford it," Annalise said, coming down the steps to give her sister a hug. Another one in her camp. "I want it to be a showplace."

"It kind of reminds me of Grandma Carrie's garden. You already have roses growing." Bridget examined the sprawling branches. "But not so good. I can fix that."

"And there are more in the back," Annalise said.

"With a little care these old bushes will be full of blooms next summer. I bet they're the old-fashioned fragrant kind. We'll have to see." Bridget walked around the expanse of yard, examining former flowerbeds, kicking at the brown grass, studying the tall trees.

"Let's see the back," she said, completing her circle.

She was just as pleased with the backyard—large by city standards, and full of old trees and shrubs. She and Annalise discussed what could be done, and Bridget was even more excited than Annalise about the possibilities.

Randy came around the side of the house. "Anyone here own that car behind my truck?" he asked.

"I do," Bridget said, turning. She smiled brightly. "Hello, I don't think we've met."

"Bridget, this is Randy Hawthorne. My sister Bridget. Randy's helping me renovate the inside of the place."

"And I'm finished for the day. See you next Friday?"

"Yes—as we arranged."

"Wasn't sure we were going to continue in light of Dominic now helping."

Annalise wanted to say *that* was the arrangement she was uncertain about, but she wouldn't say it aloud. "Dominic may have to go out of town on business at a moment's notice. I want some assurance this project will continue on track. You're hired for the duration."

"Works for me," Randy said, with an easy grin.

"I'll move my car," Bridget said, walking over to Randy and falling in step as they both headed for the driveway.

Annalise sat on the back steps, waiting for her sister. She liked the ideas Bridget had proposed, and couldn't wait until spring, when she would see the flowers in bloom.

Bridget returned a few moments later. "Wow—what a hunk. What does Dominic think of you working with that guy?" She sat on the steps beside Annalise.

"He hasn't said anything, but he sure volunteered to help quickly enough when he got a good look at Randy."

Bridget laughed. "Not that he'd ever have to worry about you. I never saw two people so in tune with each other. You can practically finish each other's sentences."

Annalise wanted to confide in her sister, but until she made her announcement to the whole family about her pregnancy, she had to keep quiet. Except…

"He doesn't think much of my remodeling project. He likes the flat we own."

"I do, too. It's so elegant, and yet comfortable." She looked around. "This is going to be a lot of work compared to no yard at all. You don't even have a balcony with flowers now. Are you sure you're up to it? You two travel so much. Though I wouldn't mind coming over to keep an eye on things."

"We may not be traveling as much in the future. And I figure we can always hire a gardener."

"I guess. Nothing like getting your fingers in the soil, however. Or talking to your plants as you prune them and water them," Bridget said.

"Is that the secret to your green thumb? You talk to the plants?"

"And encourage them to be all they can be. It works. Grandma Carrie taught me that."

Dominic came around from the side of the house. "I thought I heard voices. Hi, Bridget. What's your verdict about the jungle?"

"Hi, Dominic. You have a huge challenge here, but I'm up to it. Leave everything in my capable hands and you'll have a showplace in spring."

He looked at the tangled and overgrown yard and shook his head. "I can't picture it."

"Annalise said to make it low maintenance, so I'll install sprinklers and get only plants that require minimum care. With maybe a couple of flowering ones that might take a bit more."

"A gardener will take care of it all," Annalise repeated, with a glance at Dominic. "I want a big lawn area."

"Umm, you may change your mind," Bridget said. "Can I see the inside now?"

"Sorry—we just sealed the wood floors on the ground level. Can't go in for forty-eight hours," Dominic said.

"Come back next weekend. I'll give you the grand tour," Annalise said.

Her cell rang. She answered, looking at Bridget as she said, "Hi, Mom."

Her mother asked if she and Dominic were available next weekend, to meet with the rest of the family at the sea cottage.

"What day?" she asked, already wondering what she could rearrange with the tasks on the house to accommodate her mother's request.

"Sunday. I haven't confirmed that day with everyone yet, but so far everyone I have talked with has the weekend free," Helen said.

"I'm available Sunday." She raised her eyebrows, looking at Dominic, and he paused a moment, then nodded. It would still give her two days for renovation work.

"Is Dominic in town?"

"Dominic's available, too, as far as I know. He's right here. As is Bridget. Do you want to talk to her?"

"Yes. Plan to arrive midmorning. We'll have lunch, and then everyone can leave before dark."

"What's up, Mom?"

"Tell you on Sunday. Let me speak to your sister."

Annalise handed the phone to Bridget and walked over to Dominic. "Mom is gathering the entire family at the sea cottage next Sunday. But she won't say why. Nothing awful, do you think?"

"I'm sure she'd tell you right away if something awful was up."

She glanced at her sister, who was still talking on the phone.

"So, can you go with me?" She hated to ask, but if

he didn't go it would raise more questions than she wanted to answer.

"Of course."

Annalise wished he'd take her in his arms and kiss away the estrangement. But before she could even ask him to hold her, Bridget rose and crossed the distance to hand Annalise back her phone.

"Weird. Why won't she say why we're all meeting?" Bridget asked. "I think I'll go home and call the others. Maybe she let some clues drop and I can put them all together to find out why."

"Good luck. Mom doesn't let anyone know what she doesn't want them to know," Annalise said.

"See you next Sunday, then." Bridget hugged them both, and left.

"Nothing more to do inside?" Annalise asked. Did she have to worry about her parents on top of everything else going on in her life?

"I checked everything was turned off before we finished the floors. We worked our way to the front door. You can lock it, and we can leave. I have to go by the office. I'll be home later."

"Thanks for your help, Dominic."

"You don't need to pay for help, Annalise. If I'm not available, get one of your brothers."

"This way I can call the shots and not have to wait on someone's availability. Don't you think Randy's competent?"

"He seems to know his stuff. What I don't like is the idea of the two of you working so closely."

She shrugged.

Dominic turned and headed for his car. "I'll be home later."

"I'll be staying at Lianne's until the house is habitable again," she said.

He turned back and stared at her for a long moment. "As you like." In only moments, he was gone.

Annalise kept her days busy with clients and new listings. Evenings she spent with Lianne and Tray, trying to ignore the fact her husband had not called.

To Annalise's surprise, Dominic arrived at the house on Friday morning earlier than Randy. He told her he'd arranged for a few days off to help out, and that she should take advantage of the time while he had it.

She and the two men painted the front rooms and worked on the small room behind the living room. She was anxious to get started on the kitchen, but knew that would be such a monumental task it was best left until she had more energy. If she ever would while pregnant.

Nothing was said about their living arrangements. With Randy in earshot all day, it was hard to have any private conversation—which both suited Annalise and frustrated her.

Sunday, Dominic picked her up at the house to drive to the cottage together. Annalise watched the familiar scenery as they drove east, feeling awkward. She hadn't completely severed ties with Dominic. Yet she hoped the estrangement was showing him what he was missing with her gone. Glancing at him, she wondered if it was working. She was encouraged by his helping with the house. Yet yesterday, he could have been the hired help like Randy for all the special treatment he'd given her.

Dominic hadn't said much since he picked her up and she didn't know how to open the topic closest to her heart—literally. She wanted to tell her family about the baby. Yet the last thing she wanted was for him to tell everyone how against having a baby he was. No one would understand. She, who knew him best, didn't fully understand. She knew the past held a tremendous hold on him even today. Would anything get through that barrier?

They were not the last to arrive, but more than half the family was there when they pulled in. The day was beautiful, cold, but sunny with no wind. Children ran on the beach, staying back from the waves, but tempting fate by running up to the water's edge and dashing away when the water advanced.

"We did that as kids," Annalise said, watching them for a moment. She couldn't wait until her own son or daughter dared the water. And got scolded when they got wet against instructions to the contrary.

Her brother-in-law, Sam, was watching the kids. No one let the children on the beach without adult supervision.

Dominic looked at him when he got out of the car.

"Sam got kid duty."

"Until someone switches with him. Didn't you watch them last summer for a while when Grandpa Paul wanted a break?"

Dominic nodded.

"And was it so awful?"

"Annalise, watching your nieces and nephews for a few hours at the shore is nothing like raising a child. A few hours' duty is not a life sentence."

"Having a child is not a life sentence. You make it sound like a crime," she said, annoyed he still held that view. She walked into the house and was immediately surrounded by brothers and sisters and grandparents and parents. She hugged everyone, so grateful to have such a loving family. Dominic entered a moment later and was swept up into greetings, as well. How could he not want some of this for himself with his own child?

Everyone arrived before lunch. The food was set out on the porch, deli trays for making sandwiches, an assortment of salads, cut up fruit, chips and a variety of beverages. It was buffet-style. Chairs were brought from the house, from the storage shed and soon everyone was eating and catching up on news. Since they'd all been together just a few weeks ago when celebrating Lianne's news, there wasn't as much to catch up on. But conversations were lively and full of laughter.

Once everyone had eaten, Patrick O'Mallory rose. His wife crossed the porch to join him and beamed at the group. The silence was sudden. Siblings exchanged glances. Annalise reached for Dominic's hand. If it was bad news, she needed his support.

"You mother and I have an announcement."

"You're not pregnant!" one of her brothers called.

Everyone laughed.

"No, we did that enough times," Helen said. She smiled up at Patrick.

"Since we are having a new grandbaby in the family come next summer," he smiled at Lianne, "time to do something extravagant right now. We are going on an archeological dig in the Yucatan. We leave just before Christmas and will be gone for five months. So no do livering that baby before we return," he said, with another smile at Lianne.

The group broke out in questions and comments. Annalise sat back, feeling oddly bereft. Her parents didn't even know about her baby—and they were leaving in a few weeks for months. She had to tell them before then. She glanced at Dominic, he was studying the group's reaction.

"We'll tell you all about it," Patrick said. And he began to relate how they decided to try something new, how they researched opportunities for amateurs to help, how he was taking a sabbatical from his practice. They had been planning this for months and no one in the family had had a clue.

Dominic leaned closer to Annalise and said softly, "You are not the only one who can keep a secret."

She nodded, holding back tears. Once again she had to keep silent. She would not take away from her parents' glow of excitement. She'd tell them before they left, but not today.

She pulled her hand from Dominic's and balled it into a fist. If not for his reaction, everyone would have learned of her pregnancy weeks ago, and be celebrating it like Lianne's. If he had acted like this around Phyllis, no wonder the woman had become clingy, she wanted to make sure he'd stick around.

When her father finished talking, she stood and went to give her parents a hug.

"I'm excited for you both. What a fun adventure. Next maybe you can go to Egypt or something," she said, careful to keep her voice excited.

"We may not like it, sounds like a lot of work," her mother said. But the happiness shining in her eyes belied her true belief.

Annalise stepped aside for her brother Declan to hug her parents. She slipped off the porch and walked to the water's edge. Maybe a walk along the beach would help. She felt all mixed up, happy for her parents, annoyed with Dominic, feeling a bit sorry for herself.

"Hey, wait up," Lianne called and then came hurrying after Annalise.

"I thought I'd take a walk along the beach," she said when her twin caught up.

"I'll go with you," Lianne said, turning to head north.

Glancing over her shoulder, she waved. "I think Tray will join us, unless you want a private time."

"Doesn't much matter, does it, don't you tell him everything," Annalise said.

"Pretty much," Lianne admitted. "Unless you told me in confidence, then I'd never say a word."

"I'm not much company. Sometimes I get so angry at Dominic I want to slap him or something. Everyone's rejoicing in your pregnancy. Now Mom and Dad are doing something fun and exciting and we're all happy for them. I haven't told anyone but you about my baby, and soon my parents will be a thousand miles away and they may not know even then." To her horror, she burst into tears. "Oh, great, now they'll think I don't want them to go," she said, brushing the tears away.

Lianne put her arm across her sister's shoulders. "No one can see, they are too far away. Come on, a walk will put things into prospective. You can always march back there right now and tell them you're pregnant."

"And spoil Mom and Dad's announcement day? I don't think so. Besides, I've held off because I don't know what Dominic's going to say or do."

"So press him for some answers, wait a weekend or two and then have another gathering, another announcement."

"And if Dominic isn't on board by then?"

"What if he never is?" Lianne asked gently.

"I don't want to have to choose between a baby or my husband."

Dominic watched as Annalise went to the water's edge. Her sister went after her and the two headed up the beach, just out of the reach of the waves. She had pulled away from him after her parents' announcement. Was she upset over their plans? Maybe. She had them around all her life. And as far as he could tell, they certainly reacted differently to their children than his father had to him.

A few minutes later, Patrick walked over. Dominic smiled and reached out to shake hands. "Congratulations— sounds like the adventure of a lifetime."

"Hopefully the first of a few."

"Your children are all grown, even though Kelly and Shea are still in college. It's time to do what you want at last," Dominic said.

Patrick looked at him oddly. "I've always done what I wanted. Sometimes I feel very selfish, having my life go just the way I planned."

"Didn't having eleven children tie you down?" Dominic asked.

"Maybe having so many limited what we could do, but I wouldn't trade any one of them for anything else in the world. Helen and I knew when we were still dating that if we got married we wanted a large family. How could a man ask for better children?"

"You did great with Annalise," Dominic said, trying to ease the seriousness of the conversation. "Have you always wanted to be part of an archeology dig?"

"No—in fact, I didn't even enjoy history that much

when I was in school. I always knew I wanted to practice medicine, so science classes caught me every time. But in the last few years, I've discovered how much I enjoy learning about the past. When Helen first suggested we try a dig, I jumped at the idea. Now we'll see how much we really like it. Digging in the dirt and uncovering artifacts from five hundred years ago should prove interesting. Maybe we'll love it. Or maybe we'll long for home and the kids. This'll be the longest I've been away from them all."

Dominic thought about his father, who hadn't been able to wait until Dominic was out of the house. He thought of his own dreams when he'd been sitting on the ratty sofa he and Phyllis had owned, wishing his life were different.

And of the guilt when his wish came true.

He shook his head, still not understanding the O'Mallorys.

He and his father went years without seeing each other. Every visit was a duty on Dominic's part. In memory of his mother more than anything. She would have encouraged him to visit had she lived.

"And our first Christmas away," Helen said, joining them. She linked arms with her husband and smiled at Dominic. "My parents are hosting Christmas this year. They'll have Patrick's folks to help out, so all you children can plan to get together. If we can, we'll call that morning. But who knows what the conditions at the dig will be like?" She squeezed Patrick's arm. "I can't wait to find out."

"At least winter there should be halfway tolerable," he said.

"Dad?" Declan called from across the porch.

"We'll see you before you go," Dominic said. He stepped to the top of the stairs, looking up the beach.

"Want to go find them?" Tray asked, coming up beside him. "I could use a break from the crowd."

"Sure," Dominic said, starting down the stairs. When they were out of earshot from the porch, he glanced at Tray. "Overwhelming?"

"Do you know Lianne worked for me for five years and I never even knew she had a twin—much less ten brothers and sisters. Add that to the older generations and you have the makings of a small town. I still don't know who is who and who is married to whom."

"It takes a while. I had the advantage of knowing the siblings before their marriages started. We've been married the second longest after Mary Margaret and Sam."

They reached the hard-packed sand and turned to follow the pair of footprints heading north. The women could be seen in the distance.

"Heard you and Annalise bought a house," Tray said.

"She bought it. I'm helping refurbish it, but I don't want to live in it," Dominic said.

"We're in negotiations to buy a place out here. I have a house in Richmond where my uncle and I lived. Now that he's dead, I debated keeping it for the future, but I know Lianne would be happier with her own cottage here at the shore."

"You lived with your uncle?" Dominic asked.

"He raised me. He was my mother's brother. She died when I was two weeks old and he stepped in. He never married. I figure one kid was enough for him and he was afraid if he married, he'd end up with a bunch."

"Must have been hard to raise a child that was not even his own," Dominic said. "What happened to your father?"

"He took off when my mother died. I was kidding about Uncle Hal not wanting more children. He said he never found the right woman. I think he would have been thrilled to learn Lianne and I are expecting a baby. He was the best father a kid could have had."

"He didn't resent having to raise you?"

"I don't think so." Tray looked at him. "Should he have?"

Dominic shrugged. "Having a baby ties a man down. Keeps him from doing what he wants." He knew he was parroting his father, and that other men did not appear to resent family life. Tray's uncle had been a single man who took on another's child. Surely he'd felt there was more he could have done on his own, with the freedom to choose?

Tray laughed. "Sure it can. But only if the man lets it. Otherwise, what a grand opportunity to shape some of the future. I'll teach our child about my family history, and Lianne has a lot to share about hers. We'll take trips, educate him or her to be a responsible, contributing member of society. And get a boatload of love in return. I'm overwhelmed by Lianne's family, but I recognize the love and devotion evident in all of them. Do you think Patrick resented having so many children? He's a doctor—he certainly could have prevented any of those pregnancies if he'd wanted."

"Some men are better suited to be fathers," Dominic said.

Ahead of them his wife and her twin had turned and were walking back.

"I hope I'm one of them," Tray said quietly.

"How will you know? What if two years into it you wish you were free again?"

"I can't imagine ever wishing to be free of Lianne. And this baby is part of her. So I will always love it, no matter what."

The baby Annalise carried was part of both of them. She seemed happy enough about the situation. It was only he who wasn't. She saw it like Tray, while he kept hearing echoes of his father. He would make a terrible father. He needed to step away, let Annalise find some man who wanted children, who would make a good father for her baby.

For *his* baby. Could he step aside and let her walk out of his life?

CHAPTER SEVEN

LIANNE smiled as they drew closer. Dominic compared the twins. Despite their different attire, they looked identical. Even to the way their hair blew in the breeze. The only difference evident today was it looked as if Annalise had been crying. That hurt. Was it the thought of her parents being gone for several months? As her father had said, they'd never been apart that long.

"Are you okay?" he asked when they met.

"Fine," she said, still walking. He turned and fell into step with her.

"Upset about your parents leaving?"

"Partly. Partly about us." She slowed her pace, and soon Lianne and Tray were ahead of them. "I want to go home now," she said.

"You could still tell your parents today," he said.

Maybe he should just acknowledge he was tied for the next eighteen years, do the best he could and then be free again.

Or he could choose to end his marriage and continue with life much as it had been this past week. Long lonely nights. Eating fast food or makeshift meals. No one to talk to, to laugh with. Who was he trying to fool? He missed his wife. Only, he didn't believe he could give her what she needed.

Ending their marriage would be impossible to deal with. They'd been together since college. Shouldn't the fear of parting be stronger than his fear of the baby? Maybe there wasn't love between them? The fault lay with him. He had not loved Phyllis in the end. Was history repeating?

When they reached the cottage, Annalise ran in to get her purse and bid everyone goodbye. Dominic heard her give the excuse of being tired from working on the house. Which brought a new round of conversation as people asked her how things were going. Sean asked after Randy. Bridget told them about the garden. Dominic felt like a fifth wheel, standing on the periphery, listening to the interested discussion and wishing nothing more than that the house would burn to the ground and end Annalise's interest forever.

When they reached the outskirts of Washington, Dominic asked where she wanted to go.

"To the house," she replied.

Nothing had changed—except an added wrinkle with her parents leaving. She wasn't giving in one bit. Dominic was annoyed at her decision. Yet one part of him admired her for her stand. He had thought a night or two away would have her returning home. Or at least calling. Instead, she acted as if she didn't have a husband to consider.

"Let's have dinner first," he suggested.

"No, I'm tired. I just want to go home."

"Your home is with me, at our flat," he said tightly.

She gazed out the side window. "I'm not up to it to-night, Dominic."

Working on the house was too much. She'd mentioned how tired she was, being pregnant. She should be taking better care of herself, not adding additional chores on top of an already heavy workload.

Which she wouldn't have to do if *he* would step up to the plate. He should be supportive of his wife— offering extra help instead of adding to the stress of the entire situation.

He should.

He would.

Dominic poured himself a tall drink when he reached the empty apartment. He had no desire to go to bed this early. He wasn't sure he'd sleep when he *did* go to bed. He usually lay awake late into the night, trying to decide what to do with his life. He'd set himself goals years ago and had met most of them. Now he had another thirty or forty years of work before retirement. Who knew how long after that? Could he really see the years ahead without Annalise? Work was fascinating, but not all-consuming. He liked traveling with her. Entertaining with her. Sleeping with her. He'd never thought of the future in those terms before.

He took a long pull of the whiskey. He should end this separation, admit defeat and implore her to come back.

What if she said no?

Do you love me?

He woke early, and after a quick breakfast headed for work. At least there he knew what to expect and how he felt about things.

Around ten, Bill Patton came into his office.

"Bill," Dominic greeted him, automatically disengaging his monitor so it went black. Not that he needed to keep anything secret from Bill. He was the general manager of the security firm and kept his finger on the pulse of all assignments. But old habits were hard to break.

"We need someone in Rome, ASAP. An Italian pharmaceutical company bought an American program, have had it for four years, and now suspect someone has infiltrated and is stealing research information."

Dominic leaned back in his chair, looking at Bill. "How long?"

"Depends on how long it takes to debug it. The program may or may not have been infiltrated, but a thorough check will be needed. And if you find a link they'll probably want you to trace it out so they can apprehend the thieves. I'd plan on a week at least. Maybe longer."

"Can you get Bart?" Dominic asked. A second later, he wasn't sure who was more astonished—Bill or him. He *never* turned down assignments. The major perk of his job was the constant traveling. Yet the thought of being in Rome alone was unappealing. What if Annalise needed something?

While in Hong Kong he'd gone to the client's office and then to his hotel, with a stop at a restaurant some evenings. Other nights he'd just ordered room service. The fun of travel was seeing the sights of each place. But after five years, he'd visited most of the major cities of the world with Annalise. When he went back a second or third time, or even more, the visits were flat unless she was there with him.

"I could ask him," Bill said carefully. "Something I should know about?" he asked.

"My wife's pregnant. I think I should stick close to

home for a while." This was the second person Dominic had told, but the most important one.

"Hey—great news. Congratulations! Lucky man. I'll see what I can do to rearrange the schedules for the next few months. When's she due?"

Dominic didn't even know that basic fact. Quickly he tried to calculate nine months from when he thought she'd become pregnant. "June," he guessed.

"Then I suppose you'll want to stick close to home for another year or so, right?"

Bill rose and offered his hand. Dominic rose also, and took it, feeling like a fraud.

"I can still take trips if needed." He didn't want to cut off travel completely. But the timing wasn't right for Rome.

"Right. But only if no one else is available. Glad you told me. Give Annalise my best," Bill said, turning to leave.

Dominic watched him depart and almost called him back to change his answer. It was starting. He was going to end up staying home out of duty, envying the other men in the firm who traveled to exotic locations.

Only, the feeling he had at the moment was more of relief than resentment. He'd been gone a lot in the last few months. It'd be good to stay home for a while. There was plenty to do in the office, several projects he'd like to be a part of. And he could make quick trips around the East Coast. Was he becoming jaded about travel?

He closed his door and went back to the desk, sitting on the edge and dialing his father's phone.

"Hello."

"Dad, it's Dominic."

"Something wrong?" his father asked.

"No." It was a poor commentary on their relationship that the old man thought Dominic would only call if something was wrong. Yet how often *did* he call his father? "I thought I'd come up and see you." Time to tell his father about the baby. Dominic remembered his earlier telling about a baby, and how badly that had gone. He hoped this announcement would be better received.

"Why?"

"Do I need a reason beyond I want to see you?" Dominic could feel the tension begin. His father never made anything easy. Maybe he should forget the entire harebrained plan.

"I guess not. But I don't hear from you for months on end and then, *pow,* out of the blue you want to come visit. For how long?"

"A weekend."

"Sure—you've got that fancy job of yours that you can't leave for long. Going someplace soon?"

"Just Pennsylvania to see you," Dominic said. "I won't stay there. I'll get a hotel room. Take you to dinner." That would be one complaint less to listen to.

"You bringing that wife of yours?"

"Probably not." Annalise would want to spend time on her house, not take a weekend off to visit his father. Dominic wasn't sure himself why *he* was going. To lay ghosts, perhaps?

"Next weekend's fine. Or the one after that, too, I reckon. I don't get out much."

"I'll see you Saturday, then," Dominic said. He bade his father goodbye and hung up, already annoyed with his father's attitude. But he'd be shocked if the man ever showed any genuine delight in his only child.

* * *

Annalise felt more energetic than she'd had in a while on Monday. She was glad of her long night's sleep. And the news from her parents was more exciting the more she thought about it. She was delighted they were doing things outside the norm.

"Like mother, like daughter," she said aloud at one point, thinking of her house renovation.

She whipped through her paperwork and then scheduled two homes to be shown that afternoon. Later she worked with another real-estate agent to schedule an open house for one of the lovely homes in the north-east section of Washington that they were hoping would appeal to someone in one of the embassies. It was too large for most American families, but would be perfect for someone who had to entertain a great deal.

Her mother called to check on her, and Annalise was happy she could reassure her a good night's sleep had been enough to put her back on top of things.

"I'm worried about that house," her mother said.

"You haven't seen it. Come next weekend. We've painted the two front rooms and redone the floors and it's gorgeous."

"But at what price? I think it's too much for you. You seem tired all the time."

Annalise hesitated. She *was* tired most of the time. But not from working on the house. Should she tell her mother now?

"Anyway, the reason I called is we decided after you and Dominic left that we'd all go down to Tray's house next weekend to work on it, and if you and Dominic can join us we'll have such a crew we can complete anything he needs done. Then he can sell the house and buy the one he and Lianne want at the shore."

Annalise was torn. She wanted to help out. She loved family work days, with everyone pitching in. But that would mean lost time on her own project. She'd already missed last Sunday, and told Randy not to work without her.

"Let me check with Dominic," she stalled. No one in the family but Lianne knew she was operating under a tight deadline for renovating. It would be odd if she didn't pitch in.

"Of course. Don't you think Lianne looks great being pregnant? She's just radiant."

"Some of that is being in love with Tray and having him in love with her," Annalise said. Surely she should have the same radiant look? She was about as far along as her sister.

"True. They look like you and Dominic…" Her mother trailed off. "Annalise, is everything all right?"

"Of course."

"I was just thinking how you and Dominic used to look like Lianne and Tray. Lately there seems to be something different between you two."

"He's been working a lot—as I have. We're fine, Mom." She hoped that was true. How sad her parents would be for her if Dominic decided having a child was more than he could deal with and he left. In fact, the shock would ripple through her entire family.

"Well, then, call me after you talk with him and let me know if you can make next weekend."

"Okay—will do."

Annalise called Dominic after speaking with her mother. He was in a meeting, so she left a message.

But her afternoon was hectic and she missed his return call.

When she reached the house, it still smelled of fresh paint, and she left the door open to air the place out. She loved the cream color she'd chosen for the walls. Standing in the sparkling living room, she wanted to buy furniture right away, to furnish it as she wanted and have a sanctuary to retreat to every time she needed it while working on the rest of the place.

But, mindful of her sister's suggestion, she wouldn't make any rash purchases. If Dominic wanted furniture like they had in the apartment, maybe the living room could be that room. The little room behind the living room backed onto the pantry. Could that be opened up to the kitchen? Like a family room, where she could watch their baby while he or she played when she prepared meals?

Excited about that idea, she hurried to take measurements. She'd talk it over with Randy next time she saw him. She thought it would work. And the kitchen was so large the missing pantry wouldn't bother her at all. There was still loads of storage.

Later, when Annalise had prepared herself a light supper, she did sketches of how she envisioned the expanded room. It would open up the kitchen and give her a family room, while the living room could be like the one at their apartment.

That room make her feel serene every time she entered. There was no clutter. The paintings on the wall were beautiful, in rich jewel colors, instantly giving her a feeling of peace. The comfortable sofa looked modern, but the feel was pure comfort. The sheers at the windows filtered the light but could be opened at night to see the view. She'd miss that view, living here.

The phone rang. It was Dominic.

"My mom called today. The whole family is going down to Tray's next weekend to fix up his uncle's house so they can sell it. We're invited. Feel free to decline. It'll be a lot of work."

Dominic hesitated a moment. Annalise had expected him to say, *Sure, no problem.*

"Are you going somewhere? Not another trip!" she exclaimed. He could push away their situation by traveling. If he wasn't home, he wouldn't notice she wasn't, either.

"I'm going to see my dad," he said at last.

"You are? Since when?"

"Since this morning. I called him, and in his usual ungracious way he said I could come next weekend."

"Why do you want to see him?"

"You sound like him. Can't I want to see my father?"

"You can, but you usually don't," she said.

"Maybe I need to get some answers to the questions I have." He hesitated a moment, and then spoke again. "I may look up Phyllis."

Annalise swallowed. The anguish that hit her surprised her. She'd thought she'd become reconciled to the little she knew about Dominic's past, but this showed her how wrong she was.

"Why?" she asked.

"To see how her life is going."

She didn't like the thought, but she could come up with no reason for him not to see her. Was it just to tie up loose ends, or more? Phyllis had been his high-school sweetheart. His first wife. Was he going back to see if there were any feelings between them?

She pressed against the ache in her chest. She wanted

to tell him not to go. Had she been reading more into his help these last two weekends than was warranted?

She rose and crossed to the window over the sink, looking out into the black night.

"When are you going?"

"Friday night after work. I'll stay until Sunday."

"I'll go with my family, then." She wanted to say something—get him to invite her to go with him. Something to show there was a bond between them. Why did he need to see his ex-wife? To her uncertain knowledge he hadn't seen her in all the years Annalise had known him. Why now?

To see if he'd made a mistake in walking out on that marriage? Or to reassure himself that if Phyllis had moved on with her life, there was every reason to expect Annalise would if he walked out on this marriage? The thought made her feel sick.

"This will probably be your last family work weekend until after the archeological adventure," he said.

"I was hoping some of them would want to come to our house and help," she said slowly. "Once we're down to painting and things like that, a huge crew could sweep through it in a weekend."

She stood leaning against the sink, trying to maintain some semblance of coherency while all she could think about was Dominic going to see his first wife. And the fact he had not invited her on the trip.

"Are you okay?" he asked.

"No, I'm not. I'm scared, Dominic. We are not like we were. I think we may never be. You don't talk to me, and I don't know how you feel or what you want to do. What does that say about our marriage?"

"It's not you, it's me."

"Great—thanks for that."

She clicked off the cell phone and then turned it off.

"Go and see your first love—maybe you can rekindle old flames," she said to the empty kitchen. She'd go and help at Tray's old home, and then invite the entire family to help at hers.

Taking a deep breath, she ignored the ache in her heart and returned to the table, to try and make some sense out of the drawings she'd done.

Dominic tried her number again. Not in service. Blast it! Yet what could he say? She was right. She didn't know how he felt—he didn't know himself. How uncertain he was about this baby. How he didn't want his life to change. How he longed for her to be there for him no matter what. And how she was slipping away no matter what he did.

He wished he had the words to change things back to the way they were. But more than a baby was at stake. Their entire way of marriage was on the line. Could he change—open up about his past and offer more to his lovely wife?

Yet how could he stay in their marriage? She'd voiced what he feared—he was not man enough to be her husband. He'd never make a good father.

Next weekend he was going to his home town alone. Maybe it was a state he should get used to.

She would go with her family. It would give her a chance to spend some time with her parents before they left. And to see the house Tray had grown up in. She'd never seen the one Dominic talked about. He hoped she never did. The truth was he wanted to hide *all* the sordid past. Pretend he came from a family as loving and func-tional as hers. Never let her learn the full truth.

* * *

Annalise called Randy the next day to tell him she wouldn't be at the house that next weekend, either. "We're having a family work weekend in Richmond. My sister's husband has a home there he wants to put on the market. If we all pitch in together for one week-end, it'll be ready to be listed."

"I can work there, as well as at your house, if you like. No charge. I know Bunny is tied up, but Sean has already told her about the weekend. That way it'll go faster, and the following weekend we'll be back at your place," he offered.

"The house is in Richmond."

"I heard. It's not that far away," he returned.

It was tempting. Randy had true construction ex-perience, so if anything major needed to be done he could probably do it. "Okay, but it's for Saturday and Sunday only."

"So I'll catch up on things around here on Friday, and meet you in Richmond on Saturday morning. How early?"

"How about nine?" She expected they'd all get an early start on Saturday, drive to Richmond and be ready to go. She did enjoy family work weekends, and one brother or another was always bringing extra friends to help. "Bring all your tools," she added.

"I always travel with them. Give me the address."

Once she'd hung up from talking with Randy, she called Lianne.

"Mom told me about the work weekend. When are *you* going down?"

"Friday afternoon. We'll have everything noted that needs to be done, and be ready to start first thing Saturday as people arrive."

"Can I ride down with you?"

"Isn't Dominic coming?"

"No, he's going to see his father."

"Is he sick?"

"Who? His father? No, but for some reason Dominic is going to see him." She did not mention his proposed visit to see Phyllis. "Randy volunteered to come. He's really knowledgeable in building, and I'm sure will be a great help."

"Good—the more the merrier. We're leaving after lunch on Friday."

"I'll be ready. What can I bring?"

They chatted for a few more minutes, with Lianne referring to one of her innumerable lists. Annalise knew there would be lists posted everywhere in the house, of all the tasks needing to be done. Her sister was super-organized.

When they arrived at Tray's house in Richmond, Friday afternoon, Annalise was intrigued. This was the place her brother-in-law had grown up in. It looked so homey. He struck her as being tough as nails. To think of him coming from a regular home seemed odd. She wondered about the house Dominic had grown up in.

She got out and followed Lianne and Tray into the house. "I wish I had a real-estate license in Virginia. I'd love to sell this home," she said when she took in the room. It was spacious, and bright with sunshine. "You won't have any trouble getting it sold."

"There's so much to be done, however, to get top dollar," Lianne said.

Annalise grinned at her sister. "Nothing the O'Mallorys can't handle."

They went out for dinner and then stayed in a motel,

as Tray had already removed most of the furnishings from the house to ease the preparation. They would show the house empty and hope prospective buyers could use their imagination to see their own furniture in it.

After picking up bagels and doughnuts and coffee the next morning, they reached the house before the first of the many cars of the O'Mallorys arrived. The day was balmy and beautiful. Opening windows to air out paint fumes would not be a problem. For November, it was almost springlike weather.

Bridget arrived first. She claimed the yard, which matched with Lianne's plan. Then Declan and Sean arrived, followed almost instantly by Patrick and Helen O'Mallory and Helen's parents, Carrie and Paul. Within twenty minutes, cars were jamming the driveway and parked all along the quiet street. When Randy's pickup turned onto the street, he got the last space, two doors down.

"I guess I came to the right place," he said, walking up the front steps to where people were congregated, listening to Tray and Lianne assign rooms to work on.

There was a moment of silence until Annalise came from the house and recognized him. She quickly made introductions. Everyone was glad to have his help and expertise. Sean greeted him warmly. Randy made a comment about his sister and they both laughed.

Enthusiasm was high as everyone got started on the update. Rooms were being painted. Hardwood floors installed. The bathroom was to be renovated, with new fixtures and lights. Randy took that on, with Sean helping. Annalise drew kitchen detail, cleaning each cupboard and preparing for paint. She worked with her brother Declan and her father. Grandpa Paul was unfastening each door, marking it and carrying it outside for sanding in preparation for paint.

Lunch was boisterous, with her brothers easily accepting Randy into their camaraderie. Everyone was bubbling with enthusiasm over the speed at which the house was taking shape. By the end of the next day, the place would be ready to be listed for sale.

"I thought we could rotate tasks in the afternoon, so no one has to do one thing all the time," Lianne said. "Sean, you get to work with Grandpa Paul on the kitchen cabinets. Bridget, you and Grandma Carrie stick with the yard. Get someone else to help you. Who do you want?"

"Declan. We have some major pruning we want done; he'll be up to it."

"Annalise can help. She'll need to come up to speed to learn how to care for her own house."

"But don't have her doing anything heavy—not good for a pregnant woman," Randy said.

The silence was sudden. All eyes looked at him, and then at Annalise.

Her heart dropped. This was not how she'd wanted to tell her family. Everyone was staring, and her parents looked concerned.

"Pregnant?" her mother asked carefully.

Randy picked up on the stunned silence. "Did I let the cat out of the bag? Man, I'm sorry, Annalise. I thought your family knew."

"How do *you* know?" Bridget asked.

"Dominic told me," he said.

The crowd erupted in congratulations and why-didn't-you-tell-us comments.

"Trust the twins to do things together again—even have babies together," Declan said.

Annalise smiled and looked at her mother.

"Lianne's known for a while, but I was just waiting for the right time to tell the rest of you. Then you gave your news, and I didn't want to take away from your excitement."

"Honey, this is cause to celebrate—and it would never take anything away from anyone else, just add to the joy in the family." She quickly gave Annalise a hug, beaming. "I'm so thrilled. Another grandbaby! When are you due?"

"June."

"We'll be back by then," her dad said, giving her a hug. "Dominic's a lucky man."

Annalise nodded, but the look in her eyes betrayed her.

"What's wrong, honey?" her mother asked.

"He doesn't want the baby," she said, and burst into tears.

Dominic turned onto the familiar road where the house in which he'd grown up stood. Slowing down, he stopped the car when he drew even with it. Staring at the place, he was surprised to see it had been refurbished, complete with lush green lawn and a flowerbed beneath the front windows. It looked nothing like it had during his childhood. A tricycle was overturned on the grass near the front steps, and a late-model car was parked in the driveway. Whoever lived in the home now had changed it completely.

How much work would it have taken to make a green lawn? His mother would have loved a garden. She'd had a small vegetable plot in back, which she'd tended faithfully each summer, but Dominic knew she'd loved flowers. Hadn't he brought in his share of dandelions he'd picked? She'd always made a big fuss over his gifts. How pitiful in retrospect.

For a long time he just stared, remembering. The harsh words of his father echoed. He'd forgotten how soft his mother's voice had been. What had she wanted from life? More children? A loving husband? Or had she mourned a lost career? She had died long before Dominic had matured enough to wonder—to even see her as a person in her own right. To him, she had been Mom.

She and his father had once loved each other enough to create him. Or had it only been a one-night stand? Another fact he'd never questioned. He felt the guilt of his own failed marriage. The obsession he'd had about getting out of this town. The despair when Phyllis had become pregnant and he'd known he had to do the right thing. But the crushing blow had been the birth of their stillborn baby. Freedom mixed with remorse. Accepting the truth, regretting the longing for freedom that had been answered at a terrible cost.

Finally he started the car again and drove to his father's apartment.

The building looked old and shabby. Was this a pattern for his old man? A little effort would have gone a long way when they'd lived at the house on Stanton Street. Dominic knew his father wasn't in charge of this apartment complex, but it looked as run-down as the former residence of Steve Fulton.

Dominic parked and entered, smelling the stale scent of meals gone by. He took the elevator to the third floor, and soon knocked on his father's door.

Steve opened it, and stared at him for a moment. "Come on in," he said, turning.

Dominic took a deep breath and entered. His father looked older than he remembered. And smaller. He followed him into the living room, where Steve sat down on a recliner in front of the dark television.

Dominic sat on the sofa that Steve had bought after his wife's death. It was brown, fading a little where the sunlight hit it each day.

"How are you?" Dominic asked. For a moment, he contrasted the greeting with the ones he received from Patrick O'Mallory. As a son-in-law he received more affection than his own father offered.

"Still hanging in," his father said. He frowned. "You doing okay? Don't need anything, do you?"

"I'm doing well," Dominic said. What would his father do if he asked for help—like he had when he'd been eighteen. Probably tell him to act like a man and find his own way out of any difficulty. He had never asked his father for a single thing after that.

"Still traveling?" the older man asked.

Dominic nodded, glancing around. The entire room looked drab. There was little color in it beyond the brown furniture and the faded yellow curtains. After all the years his father had worked, surely his salary would cover a few luxuries? He had only himself to care for.

"Where have you been lately?" the older man asked.

"Got back from Hong Kong and the West Coast a few weeks ago. Before that Annalise and I were in London."

His father raised his eyebrows, then lowered them. "I never get out of town."

"And why is that?" Dominic asked. Not for the first time he wondered why his father hadn't taken off after he'd left home. His mother had died years earlier. His departure had left his father free—which was what he'd constantly said he wanted to be all along.

"Too late. I was tied down since I was just a kid. I had a family to support, remember? Didn't have money to go tooling around the world like you do."

"It's part of my job. You could have gotten another job, one that involved travel."

"Didn't have some fancy education like you."

"I put myself through university, Dad. You could have gone back to school. Face it, you had lots of opportunities and for some unknown reason you turned them all down. You're not all that old now—not even fifty. You still have time to explore new options. Why don't you?"

It was the first time he'd challenged his father on this issue. But he was tired of hearing the same old story, tired of being the scapegoat for all his father's problems.

"Didn't know how to do anything but work in the mill."

"Ten years ago, when I left, you were even younger. You could have learned some new skills, tried something different. Why haven't you done something else? You don't have to work at the mill your entire life."

"Too late. I'm too old to change."

Dominic rose and walked to the window, gazing out at the quiet street, feeling the turmoil roil inside him. "Truth to tell, Dad, you never do anything but complain. Was it so bad being a father?" Maybe he needed to get some straight answers.

"Fatherhood ties a man down. Gives him no options."

Dominic turned and glared at his father. "I don't buy that. I did for a long time, thinking everything you said was the truth. But now I'm really looking at other families, and I'm seeing that no one is grumbling all the time. They make their lives conform to their ideas, with kids fitting in." The words were hardly said before he realized it was the truth. He and Annalise did not have to end up like his parents. She'd been right. They could make their lives as they wanted *and* fit in a baby. A precious new life to keep their family going.

"You try it—you'll see. Seems to me you don't know what you are talking about. You don't have any children."

"I will soon. Annalise is pregnant. That's why I came up today—to tell you in person you're going to be a grandfather."

Steve blinked. Then a slow smile spread across his face. "So now you'll know what I meant. You'll be tied down to walking the floor at night, running to the doctor the first time the kid cries funny. Your wife will be too tired to do anything with you. So all your fancy degrees and traveling days will mean nothing."

Dominic shook his head. "And you'd like that, wouldn't you?"

"Naw, I wouldn't wish it on any man. But you come talk to me about options when that kid is in school. Needing shoes all the time—some for gym, some for Sunday best. Kids grow out of their clothes before they wear them out. You come back then and tell me if I'm wrong."

"You'll be the child's grandfather. You want to even know him?"

Steve thought about it for a moment. "Shows how old I'm getting—now I'm a grandfather."

"Time to think about the future, Dad. Go for what you want. Maybe you'll take a chance and try for a job in New York, like you always talked about."

Steve rubbed his jaw, looking away.

"What?" Dominic asked, picking up on the sign.

"Tried it once. They turned me down," Steve said slowly.

"Sometimes it takes more than one try," Dominic said, surprised by the response. But maybe it helped him understand his father's bitterness better. The one job he'd talked about, to him the golden dream, was being a set designer in New York. It hurt to hear he'd been turned down.

"Too old now."

"So try another avenue. You've always said you wanted to work behind the scenes in plays. There are plays given all over—in legitimate theater and little theater. Summer stock. Hell, school plays for that. Lots of different avenues to explore."

Steve looked at Dominic. "Now that you're going to be a father you're some smart man, eh?"

Dominic laughed. "I've always been smart, Dad. Time you acknowledged it. And me, too."

"You weren't so smart with that Phyllis girl."

The amusement died. "You're right. That was downright stupid. I want to see her while I'm here. Know where she lives?"

There were a few more things to for him settle. But for the first time Dominic began to believe that having a child would not be the end of life as he knew it. He had some serious thinking to do. Marriage wasn't only for partying and good times. It meant sticking with his partner through all life threw their way. He'd forgotten that bit. And he'd acted like a fool these last few weeks. Fish or cut bait. Stay married or end up lonely and alone—like his father. If he was so smart, that would be a no-brainer.

* * *

Saturday afternoon, Dominic pulled in front of a neat ranch-style home and parked. Climbing out of his car, he drew in a deep breath. This would be hard, but he had to do it. He walked up the path and knocked on the door.

In only a moment Phyllis opened it. He stared at her for a moment without saying a word. She looked better than he'd ever seen her. Her hair was short, curling. She wore jeans and a sweater and looked younger than she had the last time he'd seen her.

"Good grief—Dominic!" she exclaimed. Her expression was one of delight. "I never expected to see you again in this life. My, you are still the best-looking guy I ever knew. Come on in."

"Hi, Phyllis." He smiled at her exuberance. What a change from the sad, dependent girl who had clung so hard.

A toddler looked up when they entered the living room. The furniture was serviceable, comfortable. The carpet was cluttered with toys.

The little boy looked at Dominic, then stood up and brought his truck for Dominic to see.

"Not now, honey. This nice man has come to visit Mommy. Go back and play." Phyllis looked at Dominic. "I can fix coffee if you'd like?"

"No, I won't be here long. Just wanted to see you again. I'm visiting my dad this weekend."

"Sit down. I wish Ray were home. Do you remember him from school? He was a year ahead of us— Ray Stoddard?"

"I remember him. Played on the basketball team, didn't he?"

"Yes. He has an insurance business, and he stays open on Saturday for his customers. He takes Mondays off. What are you doing these days? I saw your father ages ago. He's not the friendliest of men, so I didn't ask after you."

She sat on the sofa, glanced at her son, then smiled back at Dominic.

"Nice boy," he said, studying the toddler.

"I have a baby girl napping. I hope you get a chance to see her before you go."

He looked back to Phyllis. "You're looking really good. Happy."

"Oh, I am. Lordy, I am so blessed." She tilted her head slightly. "It didn't work with us, did it? We were too young, Dominic. I was crazy about you in high school, but we were too young to have a baby, to set up house. I have never been so unhappy in my life. Now I'm so happy I worry something will happen."

"Why, you deserve to be happy. It seems everything is going your way."

"Oh, it is. I love my husband, my kids. Are you married?"

He nodded.

"Kids?"

He took a breath. "One on the way, our first." Where had that come from? First? Only, more like it.

She smiled again, then grew pensive. "It's not likely to happen again, you know," she said.

"What?"

"Being pregnant and then not delivering a healthy baby. I was so afraid when I was pregnant with Tyler. Afraid history would repeat itself and I couldn't deliver a healthy baby. But he came out perfect in every way. The second time was easier. I guess I won't ever forget our baby, Dominic. But don't let the past interfere with the present."

"I remember how hard it was being married," he said.

"I know it was." She looked around her home. "We wanted this kind of life, but we weren't ready. You had that awful job at the mill, I had the killer job at the five and dime. God, my feet ached at night. If we'd taken better precautions, we would never have been in that situation. I'm so sorry that baby died, but in the way life has turned out, maybe it was a hard lesson we both needed to learn. I won't ever entirely get over it, but I sure appreciate what I have that much more."

"Not fair on that baby, never to have drawn a breath."

"I used to think I wished it away," she said slowly.

Dominic gave a small start. "I thought I had," he replied.

Sadly, she shook her head. "We can't wish things like that. Once I got over the initial shock and grief, I knew better. Still, we could have made something work if she'd lived."

"But not the lives we each have now," he said.

"No, but something fine, I'm sure. You were always destined for great things. Tell me what you're doing now and about your wife."

Dominic spent a surprisingly friendly half hour with his former wife. Some of the guilt from the past faded as her happiness shone in every word she said. And before he left, her baby girl woke and he got to see her, as well.

He felt a wave of affection for Phyllis.

"I'm glad you stopped by. Come some time to see Ray," she said when he said he had to leave.

"I'm glad I came, too. You've made things easier for me."

She held her baby in one arm and reached out with

her free hand to touch his arm. "You were a good husband to me, Dominic. It wasn't easy. I wasn't easy to live with. You never blamed me for getting pregnant, or for losing the baby. I'll always be grateful for that. Tell Annalise how lucky she is to have you. You're still the best-looking guy I know."

He smiled at that. Leaning over he kissed her cheek. "Have a long and happy life, Phyllis."

One more stop and then he'd head for home.

He turned into the open gates of the old cemetery and drove along, hoping he could remember where the stones were. He had not been back since the day they'd buried their daughter. She was next to his mother, the only family either of them had in the cemetery. There, he remembered that tree. He parked and walked over to the stones he remembered. His mother's and his daughter's. He stood there for a long moment, studying the words on each, the small lamb that rested on top of his daughter's. Her birth had not been the cause of celebration as it should have been. Was Phyllis right, a hard lesson to cause him to appreciate what he had now.

Which was what exactly? A wife he'd driven from home. An empty apartment to return to?

"I think I've made a mess of my life," he told the cold stones. His mother would not be proud of his reaction to Annalise's news. Nor would his daughter had she lived.

"Maybe I can change it."

He thought what Annalise had said once, he was not his father. He was not a clone of Steve Fulton. He had his mother's genes in him, as well. And genes from her family. Who had given him his drive and determination?

Who had passed along the brains that enabled him to understand and troubleshoot complex software problems?

What would he pass on to his child?

Annalise sat in the living room of her sister's apartment. The weekend had been hectic. And emotionally draining from the family's discovery of her pregnancy to her stupid burst into tears. She still felt embarrassed to have had her entire family witness that. But her mother and sisters had whisked her away to semiprivacy to learn the entire story. Later she gave an abbreviated version to the others. To a person, they were surprised to learn Dominic had been married before—and no one understood his reason for not telling her years ago.

Her father took her aside on Sunday and asked if she was certain she knew what she wanted from the future. If staying married was not an option, she could always come back home to regroup.

His offer had touched her. For the first time she really considered a future without Dominic. While living for the moment, she'd always assumed they'd be together until old age. Now she wondered if that was to be. She loved her husband—or the man she'd built him up to be. He was showing flaws. Did she love the person he really was? Or did she only want the dashing man who took her around the world; who bought her beautiful things; and partnered her to parties and plays?

What did that say about her? It was the first time she spent thinking about what she wanted from the future. How she saw herself with a child to raise. What were the values she wanted to pass on? What philosophies and beliefs to share and hope her child would embrace? Could she be a part-time mother, sharing the child with a father who lived elsewhere? Or would he ignore their baby entirely, leaving the child to Annalise to raise alone?

The trip to Richmond had been well worth it from many aspects. She felt relief her secret was out and that her family had rallied around her so strongly. She'd spent some time with Lianne alone and discussed options. She'd picked up a few more pointers about renovation and had another idea for one of her bedrooms. But tonight she was not in the mood to think about all the work facing her. Her family had agreed to come for a work weekend in a couple of weeks. She'd have to list all that needed doing to utilize their labor. Lianne was a pro at that. Maybe she could get her sister to do it for her house?

It wasn't the remodeling that her thoughts dwelled on, but Dominic. What had he done all weekend? She'd called the apartment when they reached Washington, but there'd been no answer. She had not tried his cell. Was he still in Pennsylvania? Had the meeting with his father gone well?

She didn't care a bit about that—she was more worried about his meeting Phyllis again, and the results of that encounter. Why had he wanted to see her after all these years? Just when she'd begun to think he would come around, he'd surprised her and taken off to see a woman she had had no knowledge of only a few weeks ago.

Rising, she paced the living room impatiently. It was stupid to think her future rested in the hands of some woman she'd never met, but she couldn't help but worry that seeing her would change Dominic even more. They had a history together—a child who had died. Their bond was at least as strong as hers and Dominic's, maybe more—they'd shared their teenage years together. Had a similar background.

"Here we are." Lianne entered, carrying a tray with

tea and the ice cream she'd dished up. "Tray called the office and there's a slight problem, so he's gone in," she added, setting the tray on the coffee table. "I thought you'd be resting, not pacing. I'm so tired I'm going to bed after this. What's up?"

"I'm thinking about Dominic's visit to Pennsylvania. Why does he need to visit Phyllis? As far as I know he hasn't seen her since they separated, more than a decade ago. Why now?"

"You're going to have to accept that there is a portion of Dominic's life you won't ever share—his first marriage. He told you it wasn't happy. It ended soon enough when the baby died. Let it go, sis."

"He feels he's to blame. But a person can't wish circumstances into being. Heaven knows I'd wish for things to come right between us if that would work."

"Intellectually he knows that. But a baby—one he resented…" Lianne shook her head. "Imagine when things turned out the way they did. He remembered all that anger and resentment. He projected his father's complaints about life onto his own. And it all came down to a stillborn baby. I can see the guilt. Even if he and Phyllis had stayed married, I think Dominic has too much drive and determination to have remained in that town. He would have found other work, maybe ending up eventually where he is today."

"A baby changes all that again," Annalise said. "There's nothing I could have done differently. I didn't expect to get pregnant. But I'm adapting. Why can't he?"

"Personally, I'm thrilled to death about both our babies. They'll be close cousins, being practically the same age and all. I wonder what we'll have? I want a little girl, do you? Sit—eat." Lianne handed her a cup of tea.

Annalise sat down and took the cup and saucer. She sipped, placing them on the table and reaching for the dish of ice cream nearest her. "I want a healthy child. I don't much care about its gender."

She took a spoonful of the butter pecan ice cream, letting it melt in her mouth, crunching the nuts.

"Are you two moving soon?" she asked, glancing around.

Lianne looked surprised. "No. Why would we? I just moved into Tray's apartment when we married. Mine is history. But this place is large enough for us. And I love having a doorman downstairs."

"What about when the baby comes?" Annalise asked, licking another spoonful.

"We'll fix up the second bedroom as a nursery. We're buying a house at the shore. That'll be our escape when things get hectic," Lianne said.

"You'd raise a child *here?*" Annalise looked around.

Tray's apartment was nicely furnished, but looked nothing like her image of a family home. Surely Lianne had the same image?

"What's wrong with here?"

"No yard, for one thing. No family room separate from the living room, where kids' clutter could stay even if guests came over. Don't you want a dog?"

"You're thinking of our home when we were growing up. It was perfect for our family—but not, I think, for me and Tray."

Annalise looked at her twin. "Why not?"

"I like this place. There's a park nearby, and whenever we want the feel of nature we'll head for the shore. And, no, I do not want a dog. Maybe when the baby is older we'll get a cat—who can stay by itself when we go places, or come with us to the shore. But that's for the future. In the meantime, I'm just working on having this baby."

"You go to the shore all the time, year-round. Is that why you want a house there?"

"Tray and I are buying a house a few doors down from the one the grandparents own. We can stay in our own place when everyone's up, and yet visit as much as we want. And whenever I want to get away I'll have my own place, and won't have to make sure no one else will be using it," Lianne explained.

"Nice. Only two of you for the bathroom," Annalise said, remembering the long lines sometimes at her grandparents' cottage—even after the second bathroom had been installed.

Lianne laughed. "I know. That's the best part—no more standing in line. If you're really nice to me, you and Dominic can come over and use our bathroom, too."

The lightheartedness vanished. Annalise stirred her melting ice cream. "If there is still a Dominic and me. He's not the man I thought I married."

"So what other secrets can he be hiding?"

"Don't even suggest he might be," Annalise said. She put her bowl down and finished her tea. "I'm ready to leave when you are ready to take me."

"Stay the night. Tray may not be back for hours, and I'm tired. Would it be a hardship to stay here?"

"Not at all. You'll have to lend me a nightgown, but I'll stay."

The two sisters changed for bed, then settled in front of the television to watch an old movie. Having seen it a dozen times before, Annalise didn't need to pay strict attention to keep up with the storyline. Her thoughts revolved around Dominic and her fear for their uncertain future.

When Dominic arrived at the house Annalise had bought, she was not there. Her car was in the driveway, so she must have gotten a ride to Richmond with Lianne. Shouldn't they be back by now? It was after eleven. Frustrated, he left the front door and went back to his car. Turning on his phone, he saw the message indicator light and listened to his calls. Three calls: two from Annalise's brothers, and one from Tray. None sounded friendly. She had told them everything, obviously. *Damn.*

He was physically tired from the long drive, and emotionally drained from the weekend. He'd deal with the calls tomorrow. It was late. He'd wait here until midnight. If she weren't back by then, he'd head for home.

It was twelve-thirty when he entered their flat. It was dark and quiet. For a moment, he'd hoped she'd returned here after the Richmond trip, but the empty bedroom showed how vain that hope had been.

The bedroom seemed oddly empty as he discarded his clothes. In the old days, he could remember only a very few nights when Annalise hadn't been home when he was. Usually when she and Lianne went to the beach. When that happened, he missed her. Tonight he missed her more than usual.

After this weekend he had a different perspective on things. Was it too late?

CHAPTER EIGHT

ANNALISE WENT to the house early next morning, to shower and dress for work. The office would be hectic and her workload heavier than normal, with trying to squeeze in five days for every four.

She felt buoyed up by the promise from her family to help at her new house in two weeks. She hoped for good weather so they could accomplish as much that weekend as they had in Richmond.

Around ten, Dominic called her.

"You didn't come home last night," he said when she answered.

"I stayed at Lianne's. How did you know?"

There was silence for a moment.

"I went by the house when I got back from Pennsylvania. Can I pick you up for lunch?" Dominic asked.

"Why?"

"Can't a husband ask his wife out?"

Sure, but he usually didn't do it so formally. "I guess so. I don't have any appointments today."

When she'd hung up, Annalise wondered if she should have asked about his trip. She deliberately had not. At least they'd have something to talk about at lunch. She didn't want a repeat of the awkward silence of their last meal out together.

Shortly thereafter a large bouquet of fall flowers arrived for Annalise. The receptionist brought them in and several coworkers crowded around to see who they were from. The card said simply, *Love, Dominic.*

"I wish my husband would send *me* flowers," Margo said, touching one of the bronze chrysanthemums.

"Is it a special occasion?" another coworker asked.

Annalise shook her head, curious as to the reason for the flowers. She'd used to receive them a lot in years past. Lately the deliveries had tapered off. Were they a gesture of courting, or an appeasement for the weekend? What had gone down in Pennsylvania?

Dominic arrived at her work right at noon. When she met him in the lobby of the real-estate agency, he looked the same as always, and as usual her heart rate kicked up a notch. His hair was getting to the stage of needing a trim. She liked it a bit longer than he normally wore it. His dark eyes were grave. She wanted to fling herself into his arms and cling for life. But he didn't like clingy women, and she wasn't going to put herself in the category of his first wife.

"I thought we'd eat at Bacchigalupia's," he said, mentioning a favorite Italian place.

"Nice." Warily she tried to gauge Dominic's mood. He seemed reserved. Was he going to tell her something she wouldn't like? Was he trying to make it easier by going to a public place? No scene that way.

They spoke little on the way to the restaurant. Since it was a Monday lunch, it was crowded. They had to wait twenty minutes for a table. The crowded entry to the restaurant was not conducive to personal discussions.

Once they were seated, they quickly ordered, and then Annalise looked at him across the table.

"So," she began brightly, "how was your weekend?" She would not get upset, no matter what he said.

"Interesting," he responded. "I saw my father and then Phyllis."

She kept the pleasant smile plastered on her face with effort. She so did not want to hear about his visiting the woman he'd married before her.

"And?" she said when he paused.

He moved his fork an inch to the left, and then looked up at her. "It went well enough. Do you have to return to work this afternoon?"

"I planned to."

"Take time off and come with me."

"Where?" she asked.

"I thought we'd go to the National Gallery of Art. They have a traveling exhibit of Monet. The gardens at Giverny. I know you love those."

She nodded. They visited the National Gallery several times a year—usually in winter, when the weather was bad. How had she missed hearing about a Monet exhibit? He was her favorite Impressionist.

"I would enjoy that," she said.

"Then we'll go after lunch, and I'll tell you more about my weekend. I assume from the phone calls I've been getting from your brothers and father that you told your family I wasn't exactly thrilled with the pregnancy."

She was astonished. "They've called you?"

"I had three messages last night, and today Sean and Patrick left messages. Even Tray joined in."

Annalise didn't know whether to laugh at the thought of all the males in her family rallying round, or be outraged that they didn't think she could handle things on her own. She decided she needed to have a talk with a few of them—but later. Right now she was intrigued.

"Did you talk to any of them?" she asked.

"No. I'm smarter than that. But I can't dodge them forever." He moved his fork back an inch.

Annalise had never seen her husband nervous before. Her heart sank. He probably didn't know how to tell her he'd decided their marriage wasn't what he wanted, with the new baby coming. She was not going to make things easy for him. If he wanted out of the marriage he'd have to flat out tell her so.

The waiter served their order with a flourish. She glanced around at businessmen having lunch meetings, a table of women celebrating someone's birthday. She wished she could be as carefree as the rest of the patrons looked.

She picked at her linguine. Normally she loved the dish, but today she was too churned with nerves to enjoy it. Dominic seemed to have no difficulty finishing his food.

When they were done, they headed for the National Gallery. Annalise knew if he didn't say something soon, she'd explode. Even walking into the huge halls with their quiet atmosphere and lovely paintings did not soothe her as it normally did.

They followed the signs for the Monet exhibit, and soon stood before one of her favorite paintings—*The Water-Lily Pond*. The tranquil colors delighted her senses. She wished she could visit Giverny and see the settings herself.

Dominic stood beside her, studying the painting. "It's beautiful and calming at the same time."

"That's what I think." She looked at him. How many times had they walked around the gallery discussing paintings but never sharing more personal insights?

"Can you see children running across the bridge, tossing pebbles into the pond?" she asked, letting her imagination soar. One day she'd have a little boy or girl who would run and play.

"No. I see a quiet garden—a place a man comes at evening time to contemplate and think over the day. To count his blessings and vow to do better."

She blinked. "Tell me about your weekend," she said softly, her gaze still on the lovely painting.

He glanced around. There was another couple across the hall, studying another painting. He reached out to link his hands with hers and gently drew her to a different water-lily painting.

"It turned out to be more interesting than I expected. First I went by the house I was raised in. I didn't recognize the place. Nothing stays the same. Then I went to my dad's. I took a long hard look at my father. We talked, and as we did, I realized he has chosen a different way. The choices he made over the years are not the ones I've made. He says he wants out of that small town, but he's made little effort to get out. Though he surprised me by telling me he tried once for a position in a theater in New York."

"But didn't get a job?" she guessed.

"Right—and he didn't try again."

"That's too bad. I bet given time someone would have hired him."

Dominic shrugged. "I think it was easier for him to

blame circumstances than the fact he wasn't aggressive enough, diligent enough, to get what he said he wanted."

"Easier to blame everything on having a child?" she said carefully.

He nodded. "It's hard for me to talk about this, Annalise. But I'm going to. I made a vow and I plan to keep it. To me and to you. As a kid, it was hard for me to get beyond hearing him talk like that every day. It's only now that I realize my being there had nothing to do with the way he lived his life. It was just a convenient excuse. I wonder what he would have used if he and my mother had not had me."

Annalise didn't know where this was leading. Did it mean Dominic was not going to resent a child, like his father had? She studied the painting, her heart beating faster. She tightened her fingers slightly and he squeezed her hand in return. They were connected. She hoped they always would be.

"I should have told you about Phyllis and our marriage when I first met you. I apologize for not doing so," he said.

Annalise turned to gaze up at him. "Why didn't you? When we first met, it wouldn't have meant much. Even if you'd told me before we married I wouldn't have cared. But to keep it hidden all these years only makes me wonder if we are as close as we should be as a married couple."

He looked up at the painting for a moment, then back at her. "I wanted to forget. To pretend that year had never happened. Erase twelve months and act as if I came from as uncomplicated a background as everyone else at university. Back then it was important to me to fit in. To be as carefree as the other students. I didn't want anything to remind me of what had happened and how I got there."

"The death of your baby?" she said, understanding how fresh the wound would have been when he'd been at university.

He nodded. "Can you understand?"

"I can see you starting university with that attitude. But, if not when we first met, at least after we were engaged you could have found a moment to tell me."

"You were young and enthusiastic, and full of optimism. I didn't want anything from my past to dim that. And then we forged a good life together. It was what I'd always dreamed of and more. Once we began, there was never a good time to say anything—and less and less reason for it. The past was over."

"Until my getting pregnant resurrected it?" she said.

He nodded, and led her to yet another painting. They both ignored it to gaze at each other.

"Right. The minute I learned about it, I immediately remembered how much I railed against fate before. And how awful I felt about the outcome. How could anyone resent a baby? What kind of monster did that make me?"

"Not a monster. Just a teenager who was given too much to deal with before he was ready," she said, understanding how he must have felt. It didn't mitigate her own feelings of hurt that he'd never confided in her, but she could understand his emotions after the baby was delivered. "You're human. Let it go, Dominic," she said. "Forgive yourself. You did not cause your baby to be born dead."

"I went to see Phyllis this weekend," he said.

"So you said." She did not want to hear about his first wife. If he truly was over her, why resurrect the past? And if not, she didn't want to hear it. Ostriches had the right idea.

Yet one small part of her wondered at the girl who had captured his interest when he'd been younger. Was she anything like Phyllis?

"She's married and has two children. She's happy," he said.

The other couple came up to the picture. Dominic raised an eyebrow at Annalise and they moved to another room. This one held only a lone, elderly man, studying another Monet.

Annalise moved across the room from the man and lowered her voice. "You sound surprised. If you'd asked me two months ago, I'd have said *you* were happy," Annalise said. "Why shouldn't she be?"

"The funny thing is, the man she's married to I knew in high school. He always had a thing for her, apparently, only we never knew it before we got divorced. He hadn't said anything, but when she was free again, and aching over the loss of her baby, he stepped in. They were married a year later. Before you and I got married, even. Her oldest child is a two-year-old boy. She has a baby girl, too."

"Why did you go to see her?"

"I'm not sure—to get closure, maybe? To see if I remembered the past accurately? To get forgiveness for my thoughts?"

"And did the meeting give you all you wanted?" she asked. She felt left out. Not a part of this portion of Dominic's life. As Lianne had said, she had to accept that and let go of the hurt.

"More, actually. It was odd to see her so happy. I only remembered the months we were married, and how unhappy she was. She's so happy it almost made me envious. Until I remembered how happy you and I were.

After that, I ended up going to the cemetery. I'd never seen the headstone. It wasn't anyone's fault our baby died. It was just the way things happened. Phyllis was afraid with her other pregnancies that the same thing would happen, but she has two healthy children." He took a deep breath. "She didn't blame me."

Annalise felt her heart warm to hear that. She knew Dominic was harder on himself than anyone else could be. Again she squeezed his hand. "But you knew there was nothing you had done. You may feel differently, but you *know* you weren't to blame."

"I could have stood by her longer."

"Did she want you there?"

He shook his head. "She's the one who asked for the divorce. Said I had places to go that she didn't want to. Things to do so far from her comfort level she'd always feel out of step. She's happy living in the same neighborhood she grew up in. Her children will go to the same schools we did."

"And did this visit change how you feel about our baby? Are you still wishing I had never gotten pregnant?" Annalise asked, wanting everything out in the open.

"We decided long ago not to have children. Now that's changed. I'm feeling my way, here. I don't know what kind of father I'll make. But I'm willing to try and be the best one I can be."

Hope began to blossom.

"I know one thing," he continued, tightening his grip. "We need to find a way to keep our marriage going."

Annalise looked at their joined hands and wondered if they could do that. "How? It seems we have different goals."

"So we work on meshing them until we share the

same goal. I want a healthy baby. I'm sure you do. That's a start, isn't it?"

"Yes. But is that enough? When we have another crisis, are you going to freak again?"

"I know I'm not the best communicator in the world. That is going to change. This talk today is my first attempt. In the future, I want you to know how I feel, why I think the way I do about things, and for us to work through any crisis or problem that comes our way."

"I think that's what married folks do," she said.

"You asked me a question a few weeks ago. I should have answered instantly. I do love you, Annalise. I love you now more than ever. I appreciate what we have more than I have ever done. When I thought of leaving—really imagined what it would be like to live without you—I panicked. I can't do it. You are a part of my life. Without you I'm just an empty shell, like my father. He didn't have a love in his life like I do. It makes a difference."

Her heart beat faster. "I have loved you since we met. Oh, Dominic, I love you so much."

He pulled her into his arms and kissed her. The embrace went on for long moments before he remembered where they were. When he lifted his head, he was pleased to note they were alone. Had their display sent the other viewer fleeing? No matter—he'd take advantage of it. Again he kissed her.

The sound of voices coming in from the adjacent room had them breaking apart.

Annalise had a rosy glow as she smiled up at Dominic. "I was so afraid. Especially when you took off for Pennsylvania and didn't want me along. I couldn't understand why you would want to see Phyllis after all this time."

"I haven't had any contact with her since our divorce. I wanted to see how she was."

"And?"

"She's happy, like I said."

"And you are, too, right?"

"Yes. I'm happiest when I'm with you." He kissed her softly. "It wasn't right between Phyllis and me. It's perfect between you and me."

"So you'll be okay with the baby?" She wanted everything cleared up. Her heart was brimming. She loved him so much, to have him tell her was wonderful.

"I will be. I hope. I'm still worried about how I'll be as a father."

"I've never worried about that. And if you ever need any suggestions, ask my dad—he raised eleven. We're just having one."

"Maybe."

Her eyes widened. "Twins, you think?"

"They run in your family."

She frowned. "Good grief. I hadn't thought about that. I'll be huge before I know it if I'm carrying twins."

"Let's go home," Dominic said.

They turned to leave. Annalise linked her arm with his, leaning slightly. "It's okay if I lean a bit. That's not too clingy, is it?"

He laughed. "You would never be clingy. That was pure panic talking."

"Speaking of home—which? Your place or mine?" she asked flirtatiously.

Dominic smoothed her hair back from her cheek, tucking it behind her ear. "In light of my being frank and open with you, maybe you should consider that we don't *have* to have a house when we have a baby.

Lianne and Tray haven't said anything about moving into a house, have they? Our flat is large enough to expand our family."

"They're staying in Tray's apartment, but they are buying a place at the shore."

"And planning to stay in their flat here in the city?"

"Yes. Fixing up their spare room as a nursery."

"Couldn't we do that?" he asked.

Annalise pictured her house as it would be when completely renovated. And then pictured a jumble of baby things in their flat. She knew there was an inordinate amount of work to be done to make the house as she envisioned it. And Dominic had never shown any interest. How important *was* the place? It was just a building.

Not as important as her husband. Not as important as harmony and love in her marriage.

"The house is larger than the flat…" she said slowly. She hated to let the dream go.

"The flat suits us. Our friends know how to find us. We know almost everyone in the building, in the neighboring shops. We like going out to dinner on the spur of the moment, walking around the area. That house is isolated. We'd need to drive to go anywhere. We won't know all the neighbors, and the houses are far enough apart it won't be easy to get to meet everyone. And I really do not want yard work. In that I guess I'm like my dad. We talked about our house. He moved there for my mother's sake. He's happy in his apartment. I'm happy in ours—aren't you?"

"Don't you see our lifestyle changing when the baby is born?" she asked.

"To a degree. But, Annalise, think about it. We've established our routines as we like them. Travel, visiting and partying with friends. Going to the beach. A baby needs to fit into *our* lives. We are not supposed to rearrange everything for an infant."

"I think my parents did."

"They did what suited them. Do you seriously want to quit work and stay home, like your mother?"

She shook her head. "I have thought about that. I love my job. I could cut back on my hours, but still keep involved. Once the child's in school, I can work full-time again."

"So you don't want to do all your parents did? As they did it'?"

She tilted her head in thought. "No." Actually, there were lots of things she'd do differently with her child than her parents had. Take him or her with them when they traveled, for one thing.

"So why it is so important to have a house? We can make our place perfect for a family of three."

The pang of not finishing the house, of never living in the rooms she'd already renovated, struck. But was a house more important than her future with Dominic?

"I love you, Annalise. I want to be there when our child is born. I'm going to do my best to always be there, though there will be times I have to travel. But I see no reason you can't accompany me. Traveling is educational. And it's one thing you regret about being part of such a large family—never time or money enough to take the entire family on trips anyplace but the shore."

She nodded, her heart beginning to ease. She squeezed his hand.

"Tell me the I-love-you part again," she said.

"I love you. Only you. What I had with Phyllis was only a teenage infatuation. I know the difference—can feel it inside. And it's stronger than ever. I will never let you down again. This has shown me that we need to continually work to stay together, no matter what life throws our way. If there weren't people around, I'd kiss you again."

"I love you, Dominic. We were still young when we married, arrogantly thinking we could determine our future. I'm not sorry we're going to have a baby. Who knows? We may even decide to have a second one sometime along the way. But if not, we'll be a happy family of three."

"So when we throw the next party for our closest friends, we'll share the good news of the baby?" he asked.

Her heart blossomed. He'd called it good news. "Just you make sure you're there for the party."

"Actually, I told Bill to keep me close to home for the next few months," he said.

"You did?" Annalise was astonished. Then she smiled broadly. "You really do plan to change."

"Anything for you, my love. With you, the past no longer has a hold on me."

"Then let's go home."

Dominic took his wife to their beautiful flat, to show her once again how much he loved her.

EPILOGUE

Twenty months later...

ANNALISE sat on the grass, leaning against Dominic. She glanced around, smiling in delight at the flowers blooming in profusion. Hyde Park was beautiful in summer. All of London was in bloom.

"How far can he get?" Dominic asked, watching as their toddling son took his first steps on grass, heading determinedly for the bank of blossoms that beckoned.

"You can still outrun him," she said, laughing. Then a thought struck her. "You know, this is like my vision." She looked around again.

"What vision?" Dominic asked.

"When I was working on the house, and I wanted Bridget to fix up the yard, I kept seeing you and me sitting on the grass and watching our baby take steps. I thought it was the backyard of that house, but it was anyplace that had grass. Here in London, back in Washington—even at the beach, if we find a lawn."

"No regrets at not living in the house?"

"Maybe one or two. I do love our flat, you know. The house turned out to be beautiful, though, didn't it?" she said proudly.

"It did. Bridget and your grandmother worked miracles in the garden. It was the prettiest place on the block when you sold it. But you are the one who worked miracles in that house."

"I drove by a couple of weeks ago. The owners have children, and they were playing in the yard. Bicycles strewn on the lawn. A dog was barking." She smiled in remembrance. It wasn't *her* family filling the home with love and laughter, but the house held another. And that was enough for her. She had enough happiness to wish it on the whole world.

Dominic took her hand, lacing his fingers with hers, keeping a sharp eye on their toddling son. "Maybe we'll get a house one day."

"If we do, let's make it at the beach, like Lianne and Tray."

"Twin thing?"

"No, I think Grandpa Paul's place is bursting at the seams now whenever the family gets together. What with Mary Margaret's new one, and our own Dylan. Plus I love staying with Lianne—no long wait for the bathroom."

"Think they are as happy as we are?" Dominic asked.

"Yes, I do. Lianne and Tray were made for each other."

"Lucky?"

"Just the infinite wisdom we twins share in finding perfect husbands."

Dominic kept a close watch on Dylan as he made his way with utmost concentration to the bank of flowers.

"Sorry we didn't have twins?" he asked.

"Good Lord, no. Lianne and Tray are run ragged with those little girls. Though they are adorable, aren't they? And it's a good thing we had Dylan. I had dibs on the name Caroline and would have been mad when Lianne delivered four days before me."

"So maybe we'll try for a girl next time."

Annalise smiled, hugging her secret just a little longer. She knew she would not get the same response from her husband when she told him this time.

"Sean and Bunny will have a new one before long. So when Lianne and Tray come with the twins for meals at the sea cottage, and everyone else is there, we'll have to eat buffet-style on the porch. Soon we'll have to eat in shifts," she said.

"Ready to buy that house?" Dominic asked.

She turned to look fully at him. "Actually, I'd rather consider the penthouse in our building. I hear it's coming up for sale. It has three bedrooms and a den, and that lovely terrace on the roof. Think of the view we'd have from there."

"No grass?"

She ran her hands across the green lawn. "This is grass enough for me. Next week, we'll be in Rome. We'll have to find a park there for Dylan to run in."

Dominic leaped to his feet and hurried after his son, who was now some ten feet away, reaching out to grasp one of the blossoms. It would go right in his mouth if Dominic didn't get there first.

Annalise smiled. All her fears were long gone. Her husband was a wonderful father, who cherished their son in a manner that warmed her heart every time she saw them together. His fears he'd be like his father had been dispelled. Dominic loved Dylan as much as he loved her.

They had not planned on children, but now they couldn't imagine their lives without Dylan. Or each other.

Their marriage had become stronger than ever. Their

quiet time at night after Dylan was in bed was especially close. They talked about feelings and hopes and problems. Dominic had kept his vow to make their marriage work. It was blissful. She was the happiest she'd ever been.

Annalise watched the two men in her life return. When Dominic sat on the grass, she leaned over and kissed him, her heart bursting with love.

"What's that for?" he asked, keeping an eye on Dylan.

"For being you. For loving me." For the secret she'd tell him tonight, when the two of them were snuggled together in bed.

"Ah, sweetheart, you have erased the bad memories of my past and brought me the best future possible. I love you, Annalise."

She never tired of hearing him say the words.

"I love you."

Their happiness would last a lifetime.

* * * * *

*Ladies, start your engines with a sneak preview
of Harlequin's officially licensed
NASCAR® romance series.*

Life in a famous racing family comes at a price

All his life Larry Grosso has lived in the shadow
of his well-known racing family—but it's now
time for him to take what he wants. And on top of
that list is Crystal Hayes—breathtaking, sweet…
and twenty-two years younger. But their age difference is creating animosity within their families,
and suddenly their romance is the talk of the entire
NASCAR circuit!

*Turn the page for a sneak preview of
OVERHEATED
by Barbara Dunlop
On sale July 29 wherever books are sold.*

Rufus, as Crystal Hayes had decided to call the black Lab, slept soundly on the soft seat even as she maneuvered the Softco truck in front of the Dean Grosso garage. Engines fired through the open bay doors, compressors clacked and impact tools whined as the teams tweaked their race cars in preparation for qualifying at the third race in Charlotte.

As always when she visited the garage area, Crystal experienced a vicarious thrill, watching the technicians' meticulous, last-minute preparations. As the daughter of a machinist, she understood the difference a fraction of a degree or a thousandth of an inch could make in the performance of a race car.

She muscled the driver's door shut behind her and waved hello to a couple of familiar crew members in their white-and-pale-blue jump suits. Then she rounded the back of the truck and rolled up the door. Inside, five boxes were marked Cargill Motors.

One of them was big and heavy, and it had slid forward a few feet, probably when she'd braked to make the narrow parking lot entrance. So she pushed up the sleeves of her canary-yellow T-shirt, then stretched forward to reach the box. A couple of catcalls came her way as her faded blue jeans tightened across her rear end. But she knew they were good-natured, and she simply ignored them.

She dragged the box toward her over the gritty metal floor.

"Let me give you a hand with that," a deep, melodious voice rumbled in her ear.

"I can manage," she responded crisply, not wanting to engage with any of the catcallers.

Here in the garage, the last thing she needed was one of the guys treating her as if she was something other than, well, one of the guys.

She'd learned long ago there was something about her that made men toss out pickup lines like parade candy. And she'd been around race crews long enough to know she needed to behave like a buddy, not a potential date.

She piled the smaller boxes on top of the large one.

"It looks heavy," said the voice.

"I'm tough," she assured him as she scooped the pile into her arms.

He didn't move away, so she turned her head to subject him to a *back off* stare. But she found herself staring into a compelling pair of green...no, brown...no, hazel eyes. She did a double take as they seemed to twinkle, multicolored, under the garage lights.

The man insistently held out his hands for the boxes. There was a dignity in his tone and little crinkles around his eyes that hinted at wisdom. There wasn't a single sign of flirtation in his expression, but Crystal was still cautious.

"You know I'm being paid to move this, right?" she asked him.

"That doesn't mean I can't be a gentleman."

Somebody whistled from a workbench. "Go, Professor Larry."

The man named Larry tossed a "Back off" over his shoulder. Then he turned to Crystal. "Sorry about that."

"Are you for real?" she asked, growing uncomfortable with the attention they were drawing. The last thing she needed was some latter-day Sir Galahad defending her honor at the track.

He quirked a dark eyebrow in a question.

"I mean," she elaborated, "you don't need to worry. I've been fending off the wolves since I was seventeen."

"Doesn't make it right," he countered, attempting to lift the boxes from her hands.

She jerked back. "You're not making it any easier."

He frowned.

"You carry this box, and they start thinking of me as a girl."

Professor Larry dipped his gaze to take in the curves of her figure. "Hate to tell you this," he said, a little twinkle coming into those multifaceted eyes.

Something about his look made her shiver inside. It was a ridiculous reaction. Guys had given her the once-over a million times. She'd learned long ago to ignore it.

"Odds are," Larry continued, a teasing drawl in his tone, "they already have."

She turned pointedly away, boxes in hand as she marched across the floor. She could feel him watching her from behind.

* * * * *

Crystal Hayes could do without her looks,
men obsessed with her looks, and guys who think
they're God's gift to the ladies.
Would Larry be the one guy who could blow all
of Crystal's preconceptions away?
Look for OVERHEATED
by Barbara Dunlop.
On sale July 29, 2008.

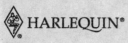

HARLEQUIN®

American ★ Romance®

MARIN THOMAS
A Coal Miner's Wife
HEARTS OF APPALACHIA

High-school dropout and recently widowed
Annie McKee has twin boys to raise. The
now single mom is torn between choosing
charity from her Appalachian clan or leaving
Heather's Hollow and finding a better future
for her boys. But her handsome neighbor and
deceased husband's best friend is determined
to show the proud widow there's nothing
secondhand about love!

***Available August
wherever books are sold.***

LOVE, HOME & HAPPINESS

REQUEST YOUR FREE BOOKS!

2 FREE NOVELS PLUS 2
FREE GIFTS!